A Tale Of Two

Ninja Kids

Book 3

Mythical Creatures Of The Forest

By Adam Oakley

COPYRIGHT

ISBN: 978-1-912720-46-0

www.AdamOakleyBooks.com

www.InnerPeaceNow.com

Published by Oakhouse Publications.

Oakhouse Publications

Contents

歡
迎

Welcome

Nunchuks

Throwing Darts

Throwing Stars

Daggers

Young Warrior

Ninja Swords

Chapter 1 - The Lost Stone

Martin was running towards the forest at night. He had left his mother and Nerris behind, sleeping silently in the house, and he was on his first lone mission to find what was rightfully his.

The ancient protective stone had been stolen from him, and now he wanted it back. Without it he felt as if something was missing, as if there was a hole inside him that needed to be filled and re-sealed. If the hole was left open, he didn't feel safe.

He approached the border of the forest, and he was holding Nerris's lost item detector. The green dot was now stationary, not far inside the forest. It hadn't moved all night.

Martin took a deep breath, and despite the warnings of his mother inside his head saying to just wait until tomorrow morning, he went inside the forest, and began walking further in.

He had never known a silence like it. It was the kind of silence that seemed to eat everything around it. Every noise he made as he stepped on leaves and dirt seemed to ring through the forest like an alarm bell. He was making himself an obvious target.

I just need to get my stone, that's all I need to do, he thought. It might have been dropped. I just need to get it back, the closer I get to it, the safer I am.

And then, just as he was approaching where he thought the stone might be, he felt something grab him on the shoulder.

Martin spun around and backed away, and standing in front of him was a girl his age. She was holding something. It looked like a big lollipop.

"What are you doing here?" she asked casually. She was wearing a dress. It seemed to be moving slightly, but there was no breeze.

Martin felt a chill wrap around every cell in his body. This looked like a ghost.

"Nothing," he said. "Who are you?"

"Who are *you*?" she said, pointing the lollipop at Martin. "I asked first."

"No, I asked first," Martin said. He suddenly realised how stupid he had been. He just wanted to go home. He felt nearly as stupid as when he abandoned Kuyasaki back in Japan, only to be kidnapped by Senzi's men and thrown into the back of a van.

"I'm not letting you leave until you answer my questions," the girl said. She sounded slightly darker now, and Martin felt trapped.

"My name is Martin," he said. "What are you doing out here?"

"I asked you that first," she said. "And you told me a lie. You said you were doing nothing. That was a big fat lie that I didn't appreciate. I don't like liars. I think liars should always be punished so that they never do it again."

She took a step forward. Martin noticed that it was not a lollipop she was holding. It was some kind of weapon.

"I've just come to get something, something that has been taken from me, that's all," Martin said. He was sure that he was only a few paces away from it.

"What?" the girl asked, edging forward slightly closer.

"A stone, just a stone," Martin said.

The little girl gasped.

"The stone? *The* stone? The stone that everyone has been talking about this evening? Oh, yes, I know the one, I know exactly the one you mean."

"Really?" Martin said. "Well where is it?"

"Don't know," she said. "Don't know."

"Well my machine tells me it's around here

somewhere," Martin said. "Very close."

He looked down at the lost item detector, and noticed that the light on the screen was now much fainter. It had almost disappeared.

"Would you like to play a game?" the girl said, suddenly.

"No thanks," Martin said.

"I like games," the little girl said. "Let's play."

"No thanks."

"Let's play!" she hissed, rushing up to Martin so that he could see her teeth in the darkness. Martin had learnt to create a space between himself and anything threatening, and he backed off to the side of her.

"Leave me alone," Martin said. "I don't want to play."

"Why?!" she screamed. "Why won't anyone play with me?!"

She sat down on the spot. Martin started to back away towards the edge of the forest.

"I just wanted to play a game," the little girl said. "Just one game."

She started to cry.

Martin had mixed feelings – fear of what the game was, mixed with sorrow for the girl who seemed to be all alone. His instinct took over, and he began to retreat towards the safety that lay outside the forest.

"I'm going to see you again," the little girl said. "Don't you worry about that."

*

Martin had begun to run out of the forest.

He could see the street lamps in the distance, and he knew he was close to safety and sanity.

Then something appeared in front of him. A large figure of a man stood there, but the head of the man was missing.

The man raised his hands to signal 'stop', and Martin tried to run around him.

The large headless man was fast. He managed to move his body in front of Martin at every turn, so Martin had to stop.

Martin stood and stared. He couldn't see any details in this figure of a man. It was just dark and silent.

The man took something out of his pocket, and Martin began to edge away in case it was a knife, or something else dangerous. Then Martin noticed

5

it was a pen, and the man wrote something down on a piece of paper.

The man dropped the paper, disappeared, and Martin began to walk towards where he had just been. He could see the road beyond the trees now. He picked up the paper, began to run towards the road, and in the very slight light coming from the street lamps ahead of him, he read what the headless man had written:

"The forest at night is no place for young boys.

Leave very quietly."

*

Nerris and Martin's mother were racing downstairs.

"Why has he gone? We told him to stay!" Amanda cried.

She slipped on her shoes and shot out of the door in her nightdress.

Nerris followed after, still half-asleep, not even bothering to put on shoes.

By the time Nerris made it out the door, Martin's mother was running up the road towards the forest.

"Wait Amanda!" Nerris called. "Don't go in!"

Nerris sprinted after her and caught up.

"You mustn't go in as well," Nerris said. "It's too dangerous."

"But Martin's in there. Something got hold of him, I saw it in my dream."

Nerris had forgotten to bring any kind of weapon.

"Wait, let me at least go and get the Demonstraliser!" Nerris said, wanting to turn back to the house.

"No, there's no time," Amanda said.

"There's always time!" Nerris said, and she turned back around to run towards her home.

"Wait for me before you go in!" Nerris called as she ran off. "Don't even take a step inside!"

As Amanda approached the edge of the forest, she slowed down. She could see something inside the forest. It looked like a large figure of a man, but she couldn't see the head. It was too dark.

She felt a rush of nerves flood throughout her body, and she started to make her way inside.

As she began to walk in slowly towards the dark figure, she saw it disappear. A small person walked up to where the figure had been, picked up something from the ground, and began running in her direction.

"Martin! Martin!" his mother cried.

"Ssshh! Don't yell!" Martin hissed. "Get out of the forest!"

"Martin!" his mother cried again, and as she cried a third time, in a mix of relief and anger, she felt something grab at her leg, snatch her to the ground, and she was dragged off into the depths of the forest.

*

"I don't even care about the stone now. Not at all," Martin said to Nerris back at her house. She had carried him home, kicking and screaming, attracting the attention of many sleepy neighbours standing at their windows.

"Why can't we go looking for her?" Martin said, nearly crawling up the walls with angst and guilt.

"Because we would just end up in trouble ourselves," Nerris said. "The night brings out so many forces that we will not be able to deal with, even with someone like the Garganfan by our side, or my Demonstraliser. We have to wait 'till it's light, and begin to ask around for what has happened to your mum."

"How long until it gets light?" Martin said.

"Two hours."

"Then we'll go. As soon as it's light."

"Yes."

Martin went and sat by the window, and he waited until the sun rose again.

Wait

No longer wait for the next moment, and enter into the fullness of now.

Chapter 2 - A New Heart

When the Garganfan woke up in his tree the next morning, he felt brand new. Normally he would wake up feeling creaky and achy, after living and fighting for thousands of years, and he would only wake up if he was called by something. But today he had just woken up, naturally, and felt as if he had been given a brand-new body. The ancient protective stone seemed to be resting on his chest, held there by one hand, and he suddenly began to remember what had happened the night before...

Jacobson Muldridge's son, Arthur, had been snatched away by a strange, gargoyle-like creature. The creature had stolen the stone from Martin, handed the stone to Jacobson, and demanded to take Arthur as payment. Jacobson refused to accept the stone, having been demonstralised by Nerris, and was distraught at seeing his only son snatched away from him and dragged off into the forest.

The Garganfan had taken the stone from Jacobson to return to Martin, and in the enormous amount of power the Garganfan felt rushing through him when holding the stone, he decided to track down the gargoyle creature and rescue Arthur.

He had been sprinting, seeing Arthur in the distance being dragged along the forest floor by something invisible. The gargoyle creature was fast and agile, darting in between trees and accelerating through gaps, so that the Garganfan could only keep it in sight, at a distance.

It wasn't until an hour passed, an hour of constant running, that the Garganfan slowed down.

He saw the gargoyle creature appear again, losing its invisibility. As it looked around to check if it had been followed, the Garganfan blended with the trees around him.

The gargoyle creature stood at the foot of a very small mountain beside a crystal-clear lake, and carrying an exhausted Arthur on its shoulders, it approached an area at the base of the mountain that was covered in vines. It stepped into the vines, parting them with its hands, and it disappeared into the tangled mess.

The Garganfan ran up, as silently as he could, and he followed in after.

He instantly heard the beating of a drum. A constant, repetitive drumming as he walked through a stony corridor that sloped gradually downward. He emerged into a large space, an underground space, where he looked down to see a whole clan of these creatures, sitting around a fire, chanting, with one of them beating a drum.

There was one creature, the biggest one, sitting on

a throne, and they all watched as one of their kin was carrying Arthur down towards them, along a spiralling path forged into the walls of their cave. As Arthur and his capturer descended, the chanting got louder.

"Bongalonga Bongalonga Bongalonga."

It got faster and faster, and the Garganfan knew he couldn't descend without being seen.

A thought popped in his head.

Should I even try to save him?

But then he saw Arthur stir at the noise of what was going on around him. The Garganfan saw a lost little boy wake up and see a clan of unknown monsters waiting for him to arrive, so they could cook him and eat him, and the terror that the Garganfan saw in the young boy's eyes made the Garganfan feel another surge of energy.

As the Garganfan held the ancient protective stone in his hand, he had a strange desire. He wanted to put it in his chest. He had noticed, for the thousands of years that he had been alive, that there was a small groove in his chest, exactly in the centre. He always thought it was normal for a Garganfan to have this groove, this little indentation, but as he touched it with his finger, he realised it was a similar size to the stone.

As he listened to the chanting get louder, he saw one of these creatures stand and begin sharpening a knife. Some of them were licking their lips, others were rubbing their hands together.

"We will be fed for days with this!" the creature on the throne cried, and Arthur was placed next to the fire, as more crowded around him, beginning to tie him up.

The Garganfan looked at the stone, which was glowing blue, and he slowly placed it in the groove in his chest.

After he did that, he could remember an explosion of blue light, and nothing else until he woke up in his tree the next day...

Now that he was fully awake in his tree, he noticed that the stone was actually lodged in his chest, and he could hear something from very far away. He couldn't hear it with his ears. It was almost as if he could hear it with his heart. Martin was coming, and Nerris too.

The Garganfan sat up, and he leapt off his tree and flew down to the ground. Normally his landings would hurt his legs slightly, but today it was effortless.

He walked to the edge of the forest, and could see Martin and Nerris running up the road. Nerris was carrying her Demonstraliser. It was very early in the morning, and the sun was just beginning to rise.

Martin spotted him, and approached him.

"My mum. She was taken by something."

"By what?" the Garganfan said.

"It don't know. She just got snatched off. Last night. When it was dark."

The Garganfan looked around. Birds were waking up and starting to sing.

"I think I know what might have taken her. Did you see anything?"

"No," Martin said. "It was almost as if this thing was..."

"Invisible?"

"Yes."

"Well let's hope to the forest that they don't cook late at night."

"What?" Martin said.

"Follow me," the Garganfan said. "I think I know where she is."

Heart

Within the heart there dwells a great and vast intelligence.

Chapter 3 - Ninja Life

For days, Myasako had been enjoying a very uneventful life. His newfound cousin Nayla and aunt Shieng had been staying with them, and everything had become very pleasant.

Word had spread that Uncle Senzi's compound had become compromised, as if a dark force had been lifted off the place. His young trainee soldiers had turned against him, and many of his guards had walked out of the compound. The police had been able to break in and capture Senzi. He was now in jail.

"I like it like this," Myasako said to his father, when alone with him on a walk. "It's nice, it's normal."

"Yes," Kuyasaki said, "but you need to expand your knowledge and skills. It is fine to enjoy the pleasantries of life, but I do not want you to become too comfortable. If you become too comfortable, you will stop learning and growing. Your training needs to go to the next level."

"Why?" Myasako said, feeling his nice pleasant life being taken away from him. "Why are you still so obsessed with me getting better all the time? Haven't I reached a high enough level? Can't I still improve here, in the dojo?"

Kuyasaki stopped walking, and stared at the Seishin Mountain in the distance. Myasako feared an eruption from his father.

"The dojo is your home. It's where you practice your skills, yes, but now you need to keep putting your skills to the test. You will thank me when you are older, when you are able to do things that people do not believe are possible for a human being to do. My aim is for you to surpass my own skills at a young age, so that I may leave the dojo to you at any time."

Myasako had a sudden strange feeling inside, a feeling that had never gripped his heart so tightly. He had always thought his father was indestructible, a man who would always be by his side. But as he watched his father walk off, with his hands behind his back, he realised that he was still just a man, a man that was born, and a man that will die.

*

"Tomorrow you and Nayla will come with me to the Seishin Mountain," Kuyasaki said. "There are tests for you to encounter there, and many of them will take place in the Shinwa Forest."

"What sort of tests?" Nayla asked. Everyone was back in the dojo. Takashi was pouring tea.

"Physical tests, mental tests, emotional tests. Even spiritual tests. You will see."

"Is it safe?" Shieng asked, looking concerned.

"Safe enough," Kuyasaki said, looking at the floor. Myasako knew he was hiding something.

"I'm not sure, Kuyasaki," Shieng said. "That's where I was taken over by that dark spirit..."

"Of course," Kuyasaki said, "which is why you might want to join them on some of their quests. You too must learn the skills to become incorruptible if you wish to walk freely on this earth. This training is not without risk, but it will prepare these young ones for a life independent from the protection of their parents."

"But they are only kids."

"Which is why we must develop their skills now!" Kuyasaki snapped.

Everything went quiet. Kuyasaki calmed down.

"Training them at such a young age means they will learn everything much faster than if we were to wait. The older they get, the slower they will be in developing useful skills. If you and Nayla wish to stay with us, you must be part of this."

Shieng looked at her daughter, Nayla.

"Nayla?" she asked.

"I want to do it, mother," Nayla said, nodding enthusiastically. "Let's do it!"

Obsession

An obsession can fuel, and it can also blind.

Chapter 4 - Bodysnatchers

"I found your stone," the Garganfan said to Martin, as the three were running through the woods. Martin had demanded that they run.

"Really?" Martin said, only half paying attention. He didn't care at all about the stone now.

"Yes," the Garganfan said. "I have it here." The Garganfan pointed to it in his chest.

"Does it help you?" Martin said.

"Yes, I think so," the Garganfan said. "It gives me power. It led me to the cave of these strange creatures last night. I have never seen them before, and I thought I knew everything that walked through this forest."

"What do they look like?" Nerris asked.

"Like Gargoyles, but bigger, more round in the stomach, even more hunched-over. They turn invisible, seemingly at will."

"Bodysnatchers," Nerris said. "They're called Bodysnatchers."

"How do you know?" the Garganfan said.

"I have a book at home," Nerris said. "I've told you that before. It has practically every mythical creature that exists in these woods."

"What do they do with the bodies?" Martin asked.

Nerris went quiet.

"Not sure," she lied. "I just know that they only snatch live bodies after they've worked for it, after they've done some sort of favour in return for it. It's shameful in their society to snatch a live body without paying for it first, and their favourite thing to snatch is a human."

"Well what did it do to snatch my mum?" Martin said. "It just took her, it didn't do anything else."

"I'm not sure," Nerris said. "But they can be cunning when making deals for bodies."

Suddenly the Garganfan felt that same flash of blue light from the night before, and he remembered what had happened...

As soon as he had put the stone in his chest in the underground cave of the Bodysnatchers, he leaped out of his hiding spot and descended through the air, landing on top of a cowering and quivering Arthur. He was instantly attacked by Bodysnatchers, and the Garganfan could easily brush them aside, making them fly into the walls of their cave around them. The more Bodysnatchers came in to attack the Garganfan, the more were thrown into the walls, and the walls started to crumble.

"Wait! Stop!" the king Bodysnatcher cried, and as the cave continued to crumble, piece by piece, everyone inside remained very still.

"I cannot let you have this boy," the Garganfan said. "It is too cruel."

"We are only going to kill him and eat him," the king said. "Where is the harm in that? It looks as if he's eaten plenty of chickens and cows and pigs himself. Why can we not feast?"

The Garganfan looked at Arthur, who was crying.

"My heart will not allow it," the Garganfan said. "I must take him away."

"You know what this means, don't you?" the king said, beginning to snarl and point at the Garganfan.

"We Bodysnatchers are owed a body! Our honourable Bodysnatcher who brought us this boy carried out a task in return for his body. We are owed a body, and we will take one as soon as we see another."

"Then I will return, and I will destroy this place," the Garganfan said. "If you take another body, you will be making a mistake."

"But how will we eat? We are sick of the rats and the mice and the small birds we manage to catch. We want a proper meal."

"I'm sorry," the Garganfan said, leaping up back to the entrance high on the wall. "I'm sorry."

The Garganfan had taken Arthur back to his father, and his father had promised to give the Garganfan whatever he wanted.

The Garganfan had asked for one thing, and Jacobson said he would begin working on it...

As Martin, the Garganfan and Nerris now arrived at the small mountain, they saw the viney patch at the base.

The Garganfan approached. He entered in through the vines, walked through the stony corridor and looked down.

It was empty.

"They are gone," the Garganfan said. All he could see was an empty firepit with some ashes at the bottom. "They've moved to somewhere else."

"Where?" Martin said, standing behind him.

"I don't know," the Garganfan said. "I don't know."

*

Kuyasaki, Nayla, Myasako and Takashi were walking towards the Seishin Mountain. Nayla's mother was following slightly behind.

"Your mother is afraid," Kuyasaki said to Nayla.

"Can you blame her for being afraid?" Nayla said.

"No. It's natural, especially since she had such a traumatic experience before. I hope this training will help to liberate her from her fears."

The group continued to walk, and began to ascend the mountain. Takashi was still constantly looking around. While it made Shieng feel reassured that he was always alert, it always made her feel on edge that he was constantly looking for danger.

The climb was easy for all except Shieng. She was not used to climbing. She had been trapped inside darkness in a cellar for years, and her body was quite weak.

"I need to rest!" she called out to Kuyasaki. Kuyasaki stopped and signalled for everyone else to stop too.

Kuyasaki made his way down to her.

"Perhaps going with Myasako and Nayla this time will be too much for you," he said. "I am eager to make you strong again, to free you from your fears, but you might need to build up slowly."

Shieng nodded.

"Are you okay for Nayla to do this on her own,

without you?"

Shieng looked unsure, then nodded. "Yes," she said. "She can protect herself far better than I can. If she wants to do this, she's strong enough to decide for herself."

"Very good," Kuyasaki said, and as he touched Shieng on the shoulder she suddenly felt a golden surge of energy flood into her legs, and then her whole body. She stood up.

"I'm ready," she said, surprised. "Let's keep going."

"We are nearly there," Kuyasaki said, and he signalled for the others to keep climbing.

*

"There must be a way to find out where she's gone," Martin was saying. He kept saying it, walking around in a circle beside the base of the mountain. The Garganfan was listening to the birds.

"These birds say they were all asleep during the night, and that they have seen nothing," the Garganfan said.

"You can speak to birds?" Nerris said. "I never knew that."

"Neither did I," the Garganfan said, touching the stone in his chest very lightly. "In fact I'm realising I can do a great deal more than just fight. You need to bear with me."

The Garganfan sat down, closed his eyes, and he entered into a trance that made him completely unaware of his surroundings. He directed his attention to the stone in his chest, and his consciousness was sucked in by a huge blue light within him, which started to yield some secrets about what had been going on the night before.

*

"What's he doing?" Martin said. "He's been completely motionless for about half an hour."

"It's only been ten minutes," Nerris said.

"How are you so calm about all of this?" Martin said to Nerris. He was reaching the peak of his panic. What if his mother had already been...he couldn't bear to think of it, but he couldn't help but assume the worst had happened.

"I don't know," Nerris said. "All I know is that all my panic and worry in my life never helped me out very much. We just have to deal with things as they come."

This didn't help Martin much, there was still a ball of panic in his chest that he didn't know what to do with. He was about ready to shake the Garganfan awake to see if he had any news.

And then the Garganfan's eyes popped open, and he stood up.

"I know where she is," he said. "Come on."

The Garganfan ran off into the trees, Martin followed after, and Nerris picked up her Demonstraliser, and followed after too.

Intuition

Intuition lives beneath the mental noise,
in the stillness of the body.

Chapter 5 - Ninja Training

"Your first test will be for stealth training," Kuyasaki said. "It can be easy to be stealthy when there are no leaves and twigs under your feet, or creatures far up in the trees to spot you."

All of them were now standing in a cave in the mountainside. It was dark, and there was a large hole in the ground that everyone was standing around.

"What will we have to do?" Myasako asked.

"You will see. This tunnel will take you to where you need to be. You will end up beneath the forest. Jump in."

Myasako hesitated slightly. There was just a huge empty hole in the ground that he couldn't see the end of.

"Do you trust me?" Kuyasaki asked.

"Yes," Myasako said.

"Then jump."

Myasako jumped in, and he felt a rush of air as he seemed to be thrown a very long distance, but in darkness, and when the air stopped rushing past him, he could feel hard ground beneath him, and he could see some writing on a stone wall ahead of him.

The writing was glowing with green, and everywhere else around him was dark and stony. The writing said:

> *To you who dare to sneak,*
> *some guidance you must keep:*
> *take your time, don't be so blind*
> *to hurry on your feet.*
>
> *If you are sensed, the creature will*
> *bite off one of your limbs,*
> *chances are it won't grow back...*
> *the creature mustn't win.*
>
> *Your task is now to seek*
> *the creature with a beak,*
> *a giant bird with golden wings*
> *who will be sound asleep.*
>
> *If you wake it, it will chase you,*
> *'till you're cut and bleeding.*
> *You must touch it on the wing*
> *without it even hearing.*
>
> *If you can sneak and touch the wing*
> *you can return back home,*
> *but if you fail you risk it all*
> *and might be left alone.*

"Do you think this is more dangerous than your father told us?" Nayla said beside Myasako. He had not heard her walk up beside him.

"Maybe," Myasako said. He knew his father was more extreme than most parents. "But we can't let fear spoil our chances of success."

And then, just above them, a little trap door opened, and a hairy little creature waved down to them.

"Come on up!" it whispered. "Your test begins now!"

*

The Garganfan had been ignoring Martin's questions for a while. He was very tuned in to what the stone inside his chest was telling him.

The Garganfan stopped running, and Martin crashed into the back of him.

"You just have to trust me, Martin, and now we have to be quiet so that we aren't detected. I believe your mother might still be okay."

"Might be?" Martin said. His eyes were tearing up with fear.

"Yes, now we are close. They went down beneath this pond."

Beside them was a small, but disgusting-looking pond. It looked lifeless, stagnant, and more like a small swamp.

Martin was now not saying anything, resisting his impulse to ask more questions. He had his mouth tightly shut.

"I'm going to swim down," the Garganfan said.

Martin stepped forward.

"Don't come with me," the Garganfan said. His voice had become very quiet.

"I don't know what is beneath there, and you need to be here with Nerris to help your mother if they try to make a run for it. Your Demonstraliser is ready, Nerris?"

Nerris nodded and switched it on.

"Very good. See you soon."

The Garganfan leapt up into the air, dived down into the green, swampy pond, and left nothing but ripples of water behind him.

As soon as the Garganfan leapt into the water, he knew what to do. He couldn't see anything, but he kept swimming down, down, down, until he reached the bottom of the pond. When he was at the bottom, he began feeling around for something, instinctively. He found a very thin rope, and began following this rope along the bottom of the pond.

He kept following it, gripping it tightly, until he seemed to reach a wall of mud.

He pushed through the wall, pulling on the rope as he did so, and his body moved through the mud slowly, not bringing any of the pond with him. Soon he was on dry land, in another cave, but this one looked much cleaner and more open than the one before.

He stepped forward, and looked down over the ledge that was in front of him. He saw them all again, all of the Bodysnatchers, sitting around a big pit, which had Martin's mother in the middle, tied up on a chair.

They were all talking to her. She was sitting there, looking afraid, but talking with them. The Garganfan sat and watched for a while, and listened to what they were saying.

"So you really thought it was clever how I snatched you down to the ground like that?" one of the Bodysnatchers said.

"Oh, yes," Martin's mother said. "Yes, it was so clever, so cunning, and so silent! I had no idea you were there, it was really amazing."

The entire group of Bodysnatchers started cheering and clapping, all patting each other on the backs as if it was a complement for them all.

"And this place," she said, "this place is really wonderful, really fantastic. The walls are so beautiful, even this pit I'm in feels special."

There was another roar from the crowd of Bodysnatchers. Each one felt prouder than they had ever been in their lives.

"So clever of you to move locations so that the Garganfan wouldn't come and destroy you all," Amanda said. The Bodysnatchers all grinned at each other.

"What else?" another one of the Bodysnatchers said.

"Your king," Amanda said. "We don't even have a king where I'm from, your king seems so fair and just and powerful, probably the best king I have ever met."

The king stood to the rounds of applause from the Bodysnatchers and he bowed to all of them.

"Thank you, thank you," the king said, placing his hand on his heart. "Untie her, she looks uncomfortable being so tightly bound."

"But the ropes are so strong, did you make them yourself?" Amanda said.

"We did make them ourselves, yes!" came another triumphant call from the crowd, and another round of cheers and applause erupted.

As two Bodysnatchers untied Amanda from her little wooden chair, she looked up and noticed that the Garganfan was looking down at her. She looked away quickly.

"Are you the strongest creatures in the forest?" Amanda said to all of them. "You certainly look it."

"Yes, yes we are," one of the Bodysnatchers said, who had just finished untying her. "There is no one stronger. No one."

There was a great sense of peace and calm in the cave. All of the Bodysnatchers were becoming so relaxed, so happy, so fulfilled, that many seemed to be drifting off to sleep.

"Well, I think you all make a very fine group," Amanda said, still searching her mind for things to complement the Bodysnatchers on. "I've never met a more harmonious, powerful and well put-together group. You should all be very proud, very proud indeed. You are the finest creatures I've ever met."

With that final line, the last Bodysnatcher to fall asleep was the king.

"You all look so beautiful," Amanda said in a whisper. "Well done to all of you. Very well done."

Then there was utter silence. Amanda very slowly stood up, and began to quietly make her way around all of the Bodysnatchers, and walked up a winding path carved into the wall, towards the Garganfan.

The Garganfan stood up, took her by the hand, and led her towards the wall of mud.

He looked at Amanda. She took a deep breath in, held her breath, and the Garganfan dragged her through the wall of mud, back into the little swampy pond, and up towards her son.

*

As Myasako climbed up the stone wall towards the strange hairy creature above him, he had a strange feeling that he shouldn't do it.

"Come on!" the creature whispered. "Come on! Come now."

"Trust your instincts. Never do anything you aren't comfortable doing," Kuyasaki's voice rang inside Myasako's chest.

Myasako stopped, and waited.

"No," he said.

"Come on," Nayla said. "What are you waiting for?"

"I don't trust it. There's something about that creature I don't like. I feel like I recognise it from somewhere, from a book I used to read."

The two of them looked up and this little hairy creature with a pale face and black eyes was staring down at them, smiling with big teeth. The mouth was smiling, but Myasako noticed that the black eyes were starting to twitch.

"Come, come now," it said nervously. "You must trust me. My name is Jozamold. Come, come on."

The creature was beckoning with its hands, but the two ninjas were not moving.

Myasako sensed that there were more of Jozamold's kind, waiting just above the surface.

There was an awkward pause, where Myasako watched Jozamold's smiling face slowly turn dark and furious.

"If you don't come to me, then we will come to you," Jozamold said, darkly, and as he jumped in the gap in the earth to land on Myasako, Nayla jumped up, grabbed him by the throat and pinned him to the floor.

Myasako heard strange screams as more of these creatures appeared above him, and they all tried to jump down at once. For a moment they were stuck, all jammed in the same gap, and Myasako could see hairy legs dangling down, some hands and one of their faces. The teeth on the face were gnashing, and they looked like they were desperate to bite into Myasako's flesh.

Nayla struck Jozamold beneath her, so that his body went limp. She picked him up by the throat and showed him to the other creatures. The one who had his face lodged in the gap screamed and retreated, and all the others copied him.

Nayla instinctively climbed out of the underground tunnel and held Jozamold's body high above her head. As Myasako followed, he took out his nunchuks and saw a whole tribe of these creatures, surrounding them, licking their lips, but looking afraid.

"Why are they backing off?" Nayla asked.

"I've heard of these creatures," Myasako said. "One of my favourite books spoke about them when I was a child. These creatures are called Herozamogs."

"What do they do?" Nayla asked, watching them all start to tremble a little bit.

"They eat skin. Just skin. But what they fear more than anything else is death. They can't help but think about it all the time, and if they see one of their kind close to death, they can't go near it. They can't bear it. They are all cowards, and they go after whoever they think might be weak and vulnerable. They have the best hearing of any known creature in the forest, and that's why they have such big ears."

"We aren't afraid!" one of them called out. Myasako could not tell which one it was.

Myasako felt a sudden urge to charge at one of them. He couldn't tell which one, until he saw one of the younger ones beginning to summon up some courage. This one was breathing harder, and its face was turning furious, just like Jozamold's had turned furious a few moments ago.

Myasako charged, with his nunchuks whizzing around his body, and Nayla followed holding the unconscious creature still by the neck.

The young Herozamog screamed and ran away, and the rest of the tribe followed. As Jozamold started to wake up in Nayla's hands, she threw him into the fleeing crowd, and he joined in, running away with everyone else.

"See. Cowards," Myasako said. "They just copy what everyone else does, hoping they will be safer that way."

Nayla watched all the hairy creatures running into the forest, and wished she had been allowed to read more as a child.

*

When Martin was reunited with his mother, he wouldn't let her go.

"How did you know to use flattery like that?" Nerris asked. They were all walking back through the forest, with the Garganfan now able to sense everything around him, as if he was connected like never before.

"There's that book at your house," Amanda said. "Mythical Creatures Of The Forest. I thought it was something for kids, but I read it anyway to pass the time. It reminded me of a few stories I was told as a child. It turns out all of those creatures that this man wrote about are actually real."

"But I told you that and you didn't believe me," Nerris said.

"No, I didn't, sorry Nerris," Amanda said. "I thought you were joking. I just remembered there was a part about these Bodysnatchers, and how compliments to them are even more satisfying than food. They can live off love and approval, but because they are incapable of loving themselves, they seek nourishment in other bodies all of the time. Until someone starts to pay them compliments – then they don't need to eat for a while."

Martin hadn't said anything. He was staying clung on to his mother so she wouldn't go anywhere else.

"I'm sorry I ran off," Martin said. "It was stupid, stupid stupid stupid."

Amanda let him wallow for a moment. Then a moment longer.

"It was a bit, yes," Amanda said. "But we all do stupid things sometimes. As long as you've learnt from it, that's all that matters."

"Well I have learnt from it," Martin said. "I have learnt to never go into the forest alone, especially at night. Also I've learnt that it might have been a good thing that the stone was taken from me, because it seems to want to be with the Garganfan."

"Do you want it back?" the Garganfan asked. He didn't want to take it out of his chest, but he would if Martin wanted it back.

"No thanks, you keep it," Martin said. "I think it belongs with you."

"Thanks," the Garganfan said. "I feel like I've finally got my heart back. I didn't know I had been missing it for so many years."

"Are there more like you in the forest?" Martin asked.

"Not that I know of," the Garganfan said. "In other forests, perhaps, but many of us were wiped out in a war many years ago. There are some that might be in hiding, high up in the trees where no one can see them."

Martin looked up, and could see all the branches moving in a slight wind.

"I still owe you some training," the Garganfan said. "Come back when you're ready. We will keep near the edge of the forest so you will be safe. Then we can train."

"Thanks," Martin said. "That would be great. And I'm going to read that book you were talking about when I get home, Mum."

Amanda smiled. Martin had never asked to read a book before. "Let's read it together," she said.

Reading

*Reading has a way of sharpening the mind
and developing the intellect.*

Chapter 6 - The Reach Of Darkness

As Nayla and Myasako walked alone through the forest, Myasako remembered the task at hand.

"The writing said we have to find a giant bird," he said.

"There's a feather on the ground," Nayla said, pointing in the distance.

"Where?" Myasako said.

"Over there," Nayla said, running up to pick up a golden feather that lay in between the leaves.

"How could you see that far?" Myasako said.

"Eye exercises. I exercise my eyes every day," Nayla said. "Don't you?"

Myasako felt slightly embarrassed. Sometimes he didn't do his eye exercises, thinking his eyesight was good enough already.

"There's another one over there," Nayla said, and the two young ninjas continued to track the large bird.

After a few minutes they both came to a small valley in the forest. They looked down into the valley, and saw that right in the middle of it, was a large golden bird, sleeping.

Neither of them said anything. The bird looked like a golden ostrich, but with a bigger head, lying on the ground, with its wings folded up over its body.

Both ninjas remembered they just had to touch the bird without it waking up, according to the writing.

So they crept, they crept absolutely silently, until they got so close to the bird that they could see its body expanding and contracting as it breathed in and out, and they could even hear a very slight snore.

Myasako inched closer. So did Nayla. As they got within arms' reach of the bird, they both started reaching out. With his forefinger, Myasako went to touch one of the golden feathers of the bird, and as he did, the bird leapt up into the air.

It squawked and screamed and Myasako and Nayla both backed away. The bird's wings were far larger than that of any bird Myasako had ever seen. They were enormous, seeming to block out the sun for a moment, and the bird swooped down towards them. Myasako rolled away and Nayla darted in the opposite direction, and they realised this bird was trying to grab hold of them. It had huge talons on its feet that were trying to swipe at Myasako's shoulders, and both ninjas began to run.

"Go in opposite directions!" Myasako said, and he ran away from Nayla. As he saw the bird turn away from him and swoop toward Nayla, he couldn't keep running away, he had to go and help.

But she didn't need help. She was rolling, darting, evading, until she voluntarily jumped on the back of this bird, and began to control it by the neck.

"Jump on!" she called, and she brought the bird back down to stand on the ground. The bird was fidgeting, occasionally squawking, but was stable enough for Myasako to jump on.

The bird leapt up into the air, high up into the air and flew even higher so that the air became cold and thin, and Myasako could feel that he had to breathe more deeply to stay comfortable.

Far away in the distance, they could see the Seishin Mountain.

"There it is," Nayla said, and thrusting forward with her hands, the bird began to flap its huge wings, and fly off in the direction of the mountain.

As the two young ninjas were clinging on to the back of this huge golden bird, they noticed its head start to move around, as if it was looking for something.

"Stay on course," Nayla said, holding its feathers firmly, but as she leant forward even more, the bird started to veer off to the left.

"Stop!" Nayla said, "forward!"

She tried to pull its neck to point in the direction of the Seishin Mountain, where her mother was, but the bird was far too strong. It had wanted to take them somewhere this whole time.

"What's happening?" Myasako said.

"I don't know, I think it's been tricking us. We can't jump now, it's too high."

As the bird veered off to the left, it started to fly even faster. Myasako could hear the rush of air being forced backward every time the bird swiped its wings down, and they could see, even further in the distance, there was a very dark mountain that Myasako did not like the look of.

"No no no, I've read about that mountain too," Myasako said. "No, I think that's the Akuma Mountain, no we can't go there, there are such bad things there, the author warned that no one go there unless they are with one of the Light Beings from the forest."

Nayla didn't know what he was talking about, but she knew that the mountain in the distance looked foul, ominous, like it was waiting for them to be dropped into it.

"Didn't we pass the test?" Nayla said. "We touched it before it woke up. Now it's taking us somewhere else."

Myasako thought about his father. He saw him, sitting back in the dojo, and for the first time, his father was worrying that he had given Myasako too much to handle too soon.

"I think this might be part of the test," Myasako said. "I think this is what my father knew was going to happen."

*

Martin was growing a new obsession in his mind. He now wanted to meet and see and understand and even outsmart every mythical creature in the forest.

"What about the author of this book, Mum, is he still alive?"

"I don't know," she said. "It was written years ago, but there's a diary he wrote, too..."

She stood up from the sofa and disappeared down into the basement, where Nerris kept all of her books against the back wall. There were books about inventions, parallel universes, mind control, and a smaller white notebook that had grown dirty and worn over the years. It was entitled "The Memoirs Of Dr Bernard J. Hoothfellow."

She took it from the shelf on the wall, and brought it back up to Martin.

"This looks like the original," she said. "You can

see this is where he has actually hand-written about his experiences."

She handed the book to Martin, and he opened it up to begin reading. The writing was from another time, beautiful and unhurried, and Martin started flicking though the book to see what happens at the end.

"You will spoil it if you read the end," she said.

"I just want to know if he's still alive, Mum, or find out what happened to him. He must have survived it all to write these books."

Martin reached the back of the book, opened it, and began reading.

"It says he's going to continue in another diary," Martin said. "Do we have the next one?"

"I don't think so," his mother said. "I have to say, Martin, I've heard stories about this man. Everyone thought he was completely mad, a scientist that had lost his mind and began doing very strange things."

"Well they must have been the crazy ones. You said yourself, Mum, what he wrote about was real. It was all true, but maybe no one believed him."

"They still don't," Amanda said. "If you were to tell anyone about what we've seen, they would not believe you."

"Why not?"

"Because...because it just doesn't seem real," Amanda said, shifting as she sat. "No one goes into the forest anymore. They've either forgotten about it, or somewhere in their minds they are afraid of what might really be out there."

"Well I want to go back. When can we go back?"

Amanda was still for a moment.

"Tomorrow," she said. "But you aren't going to find any new creatures until you've read this entire book. I want you to study and be well-informed before you go any further with this."

"Okay," Martin said. "I'll read it all and you can test me and everything," he said.

"Would you like a drink?" Amanda said.

"Just water please," Martin said.

His mother stood up, walked to the kitchen and had a triumphant feeling that at last, her son was eager to read a book.

*

Takashi and Kuyasaki were arguing alone in the dojo.

"He is my son. It is up to me what he does and

what danger he is exposed to," Kuyasaki said.

Takashi was rarely speaking these days, but he could communicate to Kuyasaki without speaking.

"You already voiced your concerns to me before they left, I do not need to hear them again," Kuyasaki said, firmly.

There was a pause, and Takashi was staring at Kuyasaki whilst kneeling on the ground. Kuyasaki was standing up, pacing up and down.

"I'm only agitated because you are still questioning me," Kuyasaki said. "It's nothing to do with Myasako being in danger. You know I do not like to waste time discussing things twice. He will be fine. He will grow and learn a lot from this. So will Nayla."

Takashi closed his eyes.

"No," Kuyasaki said, "No. He needs to do this. He needs to become free from my protection. No, I don't want you going after them either. No. Do not do it. They should be back this evening before dark."

Takashi bowed to his master, stood, and walked out of the dojo, silently.

*

That evening, as Kuyasaki sat in silent meditation, he had a terrible vision arise in his mind. He saw Myasako trapped in a cave filled with demons, with Nayla slowly being infiltrated by darkness once again, and gradually turning against his son. He saw Myasako tied up with rope, crying out for help.

And then Kuyasaki shot upright, shaken by a deep fear that he had made a terrible mistake.

He stood from where he sat, ran into Takashi's room, but Takashi was gone.

*

"Perhaps your father will come to help us," Nayla said, as they were approaching the dark mountain. She had tried to steer the bird in any other direction, gouging its eyes, stabbing it with daggers, but the bird had become hard as stone. The evening darkness was drawing in.

"I don't know," Myasako said. "He seemed obsessed with me being safe without his help. I've read, though, that this mountain is normally very difficult to reach, you have to go through a great deal of trials and tribulations to make it there by foot, and most flying creatures, or even the Navigation Troll, refuse to go anywhere near the Akuma Mountain."

"What's in there?" Nayla asked.

"Demons. Darkness. Bad creatures that the author said he could not write about in case their energy infected the readers. He said it's so difficult to reach by foot because it is not meant for humans to go there. It is for darkness only."

Nayla had sudden flashes of memory of being back at Senzi's compound, where a darkness seemed to permanently reside over her mind, making her do things she would not normally do.

"I don't think I'm strong enough yet," she said. "I don't know how to protect myself from the darkness properly. I haven't had enough training!"

She thought about what Kuyasaki had taught her over the past few days. She didn't think it was enough to face what dwelt within the mountain ahead of them, which was growing gradually larger and darker in their eyes.

Myasako closed his eyes and searched his mind. He tried to remember every page, every detail, every word of the mythical creatures book he read as a child.

He was looking for details, anything that could help them on their inevitable journey.

He relaxed his mind, eased his tension, and an idea popped into his head – a memory he never knew he had.

"A green feather," he said. "The book said that any golden birds carrying you against your will all have a hidden green feather. Pluck it out, and the bird becomes weak."

Nayla started searching around the bird furiously. Both ninjas were digging around, looking for a green feather amongst thousands of golden ones.

Myasako climbed underneath the wings, around the neck, across the belly, until he saw something green shining in the chest of the bird.

He reached out, plucked it out, and the bird suddenly lurched downwards. It started to scream. It was like an aeroplane with no engines, starting to glide downward without any power. But they were close to the mountain, so close that they might end up gliding straight into it.

The bird began to scream even louder as Nayla and Myasako grabbed its neck and started to steer it away from the mountain.

The bird was fighting but it was losing altitude, and the two ninjas managed to steer it away slightly, so that it was headed just to the right of the mountain.

"Keep pulling!" Myasako yelled, and as the bird descended and screamed again, they crashed in through the trees, the bird landed on its stomach and legs, and the two young ninjas bounced off it, and landed straight in a huge, stinking swamp.

*

Kuyasaki was running towards the Seishin Mountain. He knew something had gone wrong. Myasako and Nayla should have been back by now, on the top of a golden bird. But they were not back. He knew something had been corrupted on their journey, and he didn't know where they were.

When he had sat in meditation again, trying to connect with Myasako was difficult. He could see his son surrounded by green, by slime, struggling to get free, but there was a dark energy surrounding the entire area which meant Kuyasaki could not tell where Myasako was.

Takashi appeared in Kuyasaki's mind, somewhere in the forest, fighting off unsavoury creatures, but Kuyasaki could not tell where. There was too much darkness around him as well.

Kuyasaki needed help, he had no idea where Takashi was, and he only knew one thing that could help him.

Kuyasaki reached the base of the mountain as the evening grew dark, and he began to climb upwards. Guilt and panic were starting to fly into his arms and body and legs, visitors that he had not felt in a long time. Foolish he felt, for not being more sensitive to what was really happening in the forest. Something had definitely gone wrong.

He climbed and climbed and climbed until he reached the peak of the mountain. On top of the mountain was a statue of a man, skinny, wearing nothing but a piece of cloth around his waist, sitting in meditation.

Kuyasaki kneeled before the statue.

"Master, I have failed my son. I have sent him away for his next phase of testing, as you did with me, but I did not sense that something has corrupted the testing system. My son and my niece should have returned by now, even if they failed the test. But they are not back. I can not reach them mentally, I do not know where they are. Please please help me."

Kuyasaki bowed before the statue, and gave every ounce of his discomfort and panic away, as if it was now in the hands of his master, so that Kuyasaki felt lighter, as if the problem was already solved.

Kuyasaki stayed there for minutes, with nothing in his mind. He had been told by his master before he passed away, to only ask for his help if absolutely necessary. Kuyasaki had done well to never ask for his help up until now, now that he had no other options he could think of.

Kuyasaki didn't know what to expect. He didn't know if the statue would come to life, or if his master would appear before him. Instead he sat up, looked at the stone statue, and wondered what might be happening in the forest.

*

The swamp that Myasako and Nayla were in was deep and thick. Myasako couldn't feel the bottom, and had accidentally got some of the swamp in his mouth. It tasted worse than sewage, as if things had been dying and defecating into the swamp for many years.

Myasako spat it out, and began to swim through the thickness towards the land on the edge of the swamp.

Nayla struggled after him, and then she said something:

"Something just brushed passed my leg."

The swamp was far too thick to see anything at all underwater.

"It happened again," Nayla said. She took out a dagger with one hand, which meant she couldn't swim so easily. Myasako stopped and tried to pull her along with him, slowing him down as well.

"Okay, it's stopped," Nayla said. "I think it's..."

And then Myasako felt her arms snatched away from his, as she was dragged down into the swamp, disappearing from view.

"Nayla! Nayla!" Myasako called. He was waiting to be dragged down as well, but nothing came for him. Myasako swam his way to dry land, stood up, looked around, and started to shake off as much swamp as he could from his body. It was still clinging heavily to him.

"She's been taken, she's been taken," Myasako heard a strange voice come from the trees.

An old, ruffled, dark and round bird was sitting just above him on a branch, watching.

"It steals things, it steals things," it said. It had a chirping voice that had been made low over the years, living so close to the Akuma Mountain

"Darkness resides, darkness resides. Flee from here, flee from here," the bird said.

Myasako noticed the bird was not looking directly at him. It was constantly looking around, all around at different areas of the forest.

"They will come for you, for you, for you as well," the bird said out loud.

Myasako stared at the bird, and then looked around him again. The trees looked sick, as if they had not been nourished, or had been depressed by an energy coming from the mountain.

"Who? Who will come?" Myasako asked.

"The demons, the demons of the mountain. Many arms and legs they have inside these woods, many arms, many legs. Even reaching out further they are now, further they reach."

Myasako heard a squawk from behind them and saw the huge golden bird from before rise up into the sky, and fly off towards the mountain.

"Getting stronger, they are," the small black bird said. "Getting stronger, even stronger."

"They took her, did they? These demons?"

"Yes yes yes, took her, took her, took her they did," the bird chirped.

"How do I get her back?" Myasako asked. "She's my cousin."

"No hope, no hope, no hope," the bird said. "She is gone, the demons have her, soon she will be a demon too. You must flee, you must flee, you must flee. They didn't choose you yet, don't know why, don't know why, don't know why."

Myasako had a flashing image of Nayla being taken over by darkness for so many years in her father Senzi's compound. Perhaps her immunity to darkness was still low, after being infected for so long.

"How do I get to her?"

"No no no, mustn't do that, mustn't do that," the bird said.

"Tell me, please," Myasako said. "I'm not leaving."

The bird looked around. It had quick darting head movements, but no movement in its body.

"Climb. You must climb," the bird said. "Only way in is to climb to the top. Very dangerous, very dangerous, no one escapes, no one escapes. You need a Light Being with you, to help you."

"Where can I find one?"

The bird was silent. Myasako knew from his book that they did not dwell near the Akuma Mountain.

"It's getting dark very quickly," Myasako said.

"Darkness comes early here, darkness comes early," the bird said. "Night time soon, night time soon, you must flee before night time soon. Do not stay, do not stay."

The bird took off, flapping its wings with a great deal of effort, and it disappeared into the dark, sick trees to rest somewhere else, further from the mountain at night.

*

Takashi had been running through the forest, after following his instincts back at the dojo. His feelings told him that Myasako and Nayla were somewhere near the Akuma Mountain, and these feelings grew stronger as he ran through the trees. He wasn't relying on his own knowledge to guide him in the darkness. He was following something else, something deeper, not sure which direction his next step would take him in.

Since Takashi had become so quiet recently, he had realised a new realm of perception that he never knew existed. It was almost as if he could sense things just before they happened. Running through the forest, his legs would jump over unseen logs and hazards, his head would move out of the way of any biting insects that swooped down to feed on him in the night. Everyone knew the forest at night was a dangerous place to be, and after running for hours through the evening and into the darkness of night, Takashi could feel eyes looking at him.

Eventually he had come to be within sight of the Akuma Mountain. Takashi felt chills and tension everywhere around him, through his body and organs and even the cells of his skin, and suddenly he stopped running.

He was breathing slightly heavily. He had been running for many hours. And then, he ducked.

A huge log held by vines came swinging in to take his head off, but he was already out of the way. Without knowing why, Takashi leapt up into the air and a huge lizard with gnashing teeth came scurrying across the forest floor.

Takashi landed where the lizard had just been, and he continued to run. He was rolling, jumping, ducking, and even swinging off vines that seemed to fall from trees. He was in a complete state of stillness on the inside, sensitive to everything, not knowing what he was going to do next, being moved by an intelligence much deeper than himself.

He was attacked. Strange ghoulish creatures with big yellow eyes and flailing arms came out of the trees to capture him. He sliced through them effortlessly with his sword.

A small bullish creature appeared ahead of him, beginning to charge him down. Takashi jumped on top of the creature and began to steer it off towards the Akuma Mountain in the distance. As he held on to the back of this small but muscled creature, Takashi continued to slice through anything that threatened his life, as the middle of the night began to draw closer in.

Faith

*Faith is knowing the reality of things,
before they even materialise.*

Chapter 7 - A Mythical Student

The next day, Martin was ready for his test. He was sat at the breakfast table, with a pen and paper, and the full Mythical Creatures Of The Forest book was sitting closed in front of him. It was quite a large book, brown and worn, but with pristine golden letters on the front.

His mother came downstairs.

"Ready for testing," Martin said. "Anything, ask me anything Mum. Will my test be verbal or written?"

Amanda was still not fully awake. She began to rub her head.

"Um...verbal," she said. "Hang on, Martin."

She disappeared into the kitchen for a few minutes, and returned with a hot cup of tea. She was still in her dressing gown.

She sat down beside Martin at the table, and angled her chair to face him.

She reached for the book, and opened it at a random page.

"Okay," she said, sipping her tea and putting it on the table. "What must you never do if you are ever confronted by a Piggen?"

"Talk about his family, never talk about his family."

"Correct," his mother said. She turned a page.

"Name one of the most untrustworthy creatures in the forest."

"A Shapeshifter. Never trust a Shapeshifter," Martin said.

"Correct. What does the Navigation Troll use as fuel for transporting his clients?"

"Pain from past memories," Martin said.

"Correct. How would you summon a Navigation Troll?"

"Touch a tree with both hands, or one hand if you are with someone else, and then hold the memory in your mind and say 'I give this memory to the Navigation Troll'."

"Correct." Amanda flicked through some more pages at random.

"If you find yourself confronted by a Nightbug, should you offer it help or try to escape?"

"Offer help. Always offer it help."

"Is Mr Lyons good or bad?"

"Good, as long as you are friendly towards the forest."

"When was the last known sighting of an Earthman recorded outside the forest?"

"Thirty years ago, in June."

"If you see a light in the forest that has a delicious pull about it, a light that you want to stare at and gravitate towards, what should you do?"

"Remember it is a Feasting Tree, and to back away very slowly, looking away from the light."

Amanda paused, as if something touched her memory.

"What's the word of safety towards all Elnoks, to show you come in peace?"

"Galash-namakna."

"Very good. What should you do if you see a Planting Bear?"

"Leave it alone, back away peacefully with your hands in the air."

"Is the Mountain Man a friend or a foe?"

"A friend, unless you upset his friends."

"If you ever find yourself injured in the forest, where should you go?"

"The Healing Garden, using the Navigation Troll's services if you have no other option."

"What should you do if you see a Dundenbeast?"

"Clear your mind of all thought."

"Okay," she said, "What is the role of Heelog?"

"He runs through the forest incessantly, finding anything sick or injured so he can heal it and keep on running," Martin said.

"Good. Have you read up on the creatures of the night?" she asked.

"Yes," Martin said, remorsefully.

"The Headless Man, what does he do?"

"He looks out for people. He warns people about going into the forest at night, so that what happened to him won't happen to them."

"The girl who you said you met in the forest. Who is she?"

"Her name is Elisa. If you agree to play a game with her, she traps you in an unseen spirit realm until she gets tired of playing the game with you."

"What about creeper vines? What do they do?"

"They hold you to the ground until you turn into a tree."

"What about the Moonsmiler?"

"He tries to make you laugh."

"Why?"

"It makes him feel happy."

"And what if he makes you laugh?"

"You might not be able to stop, ever."

"So what must you do if you ever see him?"

"Don't look at him, and make sure you talk over him so you can't hear him. And run away, because he hates to run."

"Okay. And lastly, what about Light Beings, where can you find them?"

Martin paused and looked around at the ground, furtively. He wasn't sure. He couldn't remember where you would find a Light Being.

"I thought...I thought they showed up by themselves. Some people think they respond to calls, heartfelt calls for help. They are usually creatures who realised their immortality while they were still alive, so when their body died, their spirit stayed conscious and powerful."

Amanda snapped the book shut.

"Very good. I think you've passed, but I might ask you some more questions on the way to the forest, just to make sure you know everything. Well done Martin. Your work has paid off."

Martin sat back in his chair, pleased that he had done so well. He wanted to start writing his own book, about all the mythical creatures he was soon to meet.

*

"How would I write a book?" Martin asked his mother as he, she and Nerris were walking up the road towards the forest.

"Just start," his mother said.

"With what?"

"I don't know, Martin, just make a start."

"But I don't know how. What should I actually start with?"

"It doesn't matter," Nerris chimed in. "Just start writing, anything. It doesn't have to be good, it doesn't have to be final, just make a start. It's the same with everything, if you just make a start on something without trying to figure it all out in advance, things will become easier."

"Okay," Martin said. "I will start it this evening."

"Great," his mother said. It seemed that going to the forest was turning Martin into a different person, one that wanted to read and study and write about his experiences.

And he was about to learn more on how to fight.

As the three of them approached the forest, the Garganfan was already there, waiting for them.

"I heard you coming," he said.

"Where will we go first?" Martin said.

"Nowhere. We aren't going on any more adventures until I'm satisfied that you can adequately defend yourself. The next few weeks at least will just be me and you training, developing those skills of yours."

"Kuyasaki told me I needed a good trainer," Martin said. "He taught me about consistency, and the basics of blocking punches and things like that."

"We can train these aspects, develop your fighting skills," the Garganfan said, "and if you like, take your mentality to a new level, where you can start to develop skills that people don't think are possible."

"You mean like a real ninja?" Martin said. "I'm sure Kuyasaki, the man who gave me that stone, had some kind of magical powers, but he wasn't telling me about them."

"Probably because you would have become too transfixed with the end goal, not wanting to do what it takes to get there. The end result is the by-product of the work that you will put in."

The Garganfan paused and looked at Martin. The stone in the Garganfan's chest was glowing a mild blue.

"How's your fitness?" the Garganfan asked.

"Not great," Martin said. "I still can't run very far."

"Then we will begin with running, just within the perimeter of these forests where only the birds and insects dwell. Let's go. Amanda and Nerris, you are welcome to join us."

Nerris started running after the Garganfan, always keen to train her skills in any way. Martin began running too, and Amanda sighed, slowly beginning to jog after the group.

As Martin ran alongside the Garganfan, narrowly avoiding tripping over branches and ruts in the ground, the Garganfan began to talk to him.

"What style would you like to emulate, as a

fighter? Do you even want a style of fighting?"

"Ninja style," Martin said. "Like Kuyasaki. If I could, I'd want to be able to fight like him. He made everything look so easy."

"Do you know how he made it look easy?" the Garganfan said.

"How?" Martin said.

"He just practiced. A lot. It wasn't easy the first time, or the first thousand times, but gradually it got easy, because he did it regularly."

"You don't know him, do you?" Martin said. "You sound like you do. Have you ever met him?"

"No. But I think I met his master," the Garganfan said. "His master once told me that he had an apprentice named Kuyasaki."

"How?" Martin said. "Were you in Japan?"

The Garganfan cast his mind back, as if he was looking back thousands of years.

"I can't remember," the Garganfan said, "but this master was no ordinary man. He could travel as if he was a pure spirit, to anywhere he wanted to be. I fought alongside him once in battle, and he made short work of anyone who came near him."

"See how you are running now?" the Garganfan

said. "You are heavy and clunky, all the force is going into your joints. Try landing on the ball of your foot, and see how much lighter you become."

Martin tried landing on the ball of his foot instead of slamming his heel onto the ground.

"That's harder to do," Martin said.

"Only because you're not used to it," the Garganfan said. "It will strengthen the lower part of your legs if you run like that, and it will make you far less detectable if you start to practice it."

Martin looked back. Nerris was now carrying his mother over her shoulder. His mother was not used to running, or doing any exercise at all.

After a while they came back to their original position, where they had met the Garganfan before beginning their run.

"We are back?" Martin said. "I don't remember us turning around."

"It was subtle," the Garganfan said. "You will notice changes the more you get to know the forest, the less you are in your own head, and the more you are one with nature. Now, let me see what you are like at fighting."

Martin put his hands up, and the Garganfan charged towards him.

Consistency

Consistency is a humble ally that will take you to greatness.

Chapter 8 - The Akuma Mountain

As Myasako crept slowly through the forest, realising that there were things watching him, surrounding him in the darkness of the trees that he could not see, he heard something flapping behind him.

He ducked and turned, and saw that it was the same small black bird from before.

"I must follow you. You need help, you need help," the bird said. "You don't listen, don't listen to me but I will help."

"Thanks," Myasako said. He could feel a chill in the air which seemed to reach underneath his skin. "So I have to climb the mountain?"

"Worried, worried I am for you," the bird said. "They get you, then they get stronger, very strong they will become."

"But they already have Nayla, they will be stronger if they keep her."

"Too late, too late for her," the bird said. "Let her go, let her go."

"I can't," Myasako said, "I have to help her. I know there aren't any Light Beings around here to help me, are there? If not then I have to go alone."

The bird was silent again. And then it spoke as the air around them grew colder and more eyes began to watch them.

"Climb to top, jump in through top, jump in through top. I can't leave the trees, too exposed, too exposed I will be," the bird said.

"Okay," Myasako said. "What do I need to look out for on the way?"

"Woodland creatures snapping at feet. You must not creep, or they will catch you. You must run. You must run to the base of the mountain and run up, up the mountain. Don't stop running. If you stop, they will catch you."

Myasako began to run. The bird began to fly behind him.

Myasako felt a fear, a sense of abandonment that seemed to mask his ninja skills. He had never known darkness and creatures like this.

"Jump!" the bird screamed.

Myasako jumped, and narrowly avoided falling down a small chasm in the ground that he hadn't seen. Fear was getting the better of him. He was becoming like a normal person.

"Duck!" the bird screamed. Myasako ducked as he saw a large shadow of a claw swipe above him, just missing his head.

Myasako wasn't sure if he could do this. Something was inside him now, making him doubt himself and his abilities.

"No turning back now!" the bird said. "The ones behind will catch you, you must keep going!" Myasako could see the mountain in the distance, gradually getting closer, looming over him and making his heart feel as if it was turning black and heavy. He was slowing down.

"Keep running, must keep running! Must believe!" the bird squawked.

And then Myasako stopped. He didn't want to get closer to the mountain now. There was something terrible inside of it, and just as he stopped, the bird stopped too.

"Mistake, mistake, mistake!" the bird said, and then the ground suddenly opened up, and Myasako was falling through an empty darkness that seemed to have no end.

*

As Takashi continued to run through a dark forest, he began to slow down, instinctively. He could see a chasm in the ground, and his attention was drawn to it.

"Boy needs help, boy needs help," a voice from a tree said. Takashi could not see where it was coming from, but his hearing told him which branch the voice was located at.

"Boy needs help, I can not go, boy needs help," the voice said again.

"What's down there?" Takashi thought.

"Dreadful things. The rejects of the mountain. Worst of the worst. He needs help, needs Light Being but none are here."

Takashi looked around to sense if he was being watched by anything else. He felt that the walls of the chasm in the ground were rough and jagged, and he began to climb down them, to find Myasako.

As Takashi descended, he could hear dark cackling. It seemed blacker than black down there, and Takashi could no longer see the wall in front of his face as he climbed down. He went inside himself, and demanded that his eyes become night-seeing. He opened them, and in the greyness that used to be darkness, he could see Myasako at the bottom of the cave, tied up in some kind of strange, ethereal rope.

Takashi slowly climbed down further.

"What shall we do?" a terrible, desperate voice

spluttered. "We could take it to the master to try to get our places back at his side."

"No," another voice said. "No! We could feed off his soul for years if we just keep him to ourselves. Let's just keep him to ourselves!"

"But I want my place in the mountain back! I hate it down here!" the first voice said.

"You've always hated everything, you hated it in there too! That's why you tried to destroy the master!"

"No!"

"Yes!"

"No!"

The two evil spirits at the bottom of the chasm became distracted and argued ferociously amongst themselves, as Takashi watched Myasako attempting to break free from the ropes. But the ropes had a dark magic over them that Myasako did not know how to break free from, and his growing fear was not helping him in the least.

Takashi decided to speak to Myasako from where he was on the wall. But he did not use his voice. He sent his thoughts into Myasako's head, and watched as Myasako listened.

As Myasako sat, struggling, he could feel an idea trying to reach him. His struggle kept it away for a while, and then he relaxed slightly, and let the idea enter into him. It was Takashi's voice, a voice he had rarely heard recently. Takashi's voice said:

"Evil forces do not like to be around love."

Myasako started to struggle again, and then realised what Takashi's voice was saying.

Myasako thought he would try an experiment as the evil spirits argued. He had a terrible feeling around his waist of being held to the ground by ropes that he couldn't see. The ropes felt like dark forces instead of fabric, and Myasako had been hating them since he became trapped. Every time he hated the darkness, it grew stronger. So he decided to change his attitude.

"I welcome these ropes," he said within himself, and as soon as he said that, he felt their grip weaken slightly.

"I welcome these ropes," he said again. He felt it, as part of his experiment, as strongly as he could. He then decided he would begin to love these ropes as if he wanted them to actually be there.

Gradually their hold over him began to weaken, and he could feel his body becoming free.

"I love every part of these ropes and I wish they

would stay with me forever," he thought.

And at that final word within his own mind, the hold over him dropped, and he began to tip-toe his way towards the wall, where he knew he could begin climbing.

"Stay in that state, or you will become susceptible again," Takashi's voice said in his head, and in a state of loving embrace, and without any presence of fear of the darkness, Myasako began to climb the wall, and make his escape.

*

As soon as Nayla had been snatched down from the surface of the swamp, she could feel something wrapped tightly around her leg. She couldn't see anything, but took a dagger out from her belt and thrust it into whatever had a hold on her.

She heard an underground scream that rippled through her body, and as soon as she was released, something else wrapped around her arm and continued to pull her down. She continued to slash at whatever held her, but she was continually re-seized until she was ejected from the swamp and thrown into what looked like an underground dungeon.

The walls were tinged with red.

She heard something laughing, something so dark

and powerful it made her stand up and look for an exit.

"You are a powerful one, my dear, we could use you."

Nayla didn't say anything. She was looking around to see what appeared.

As she stared ahead, an old man using a crooked walking stick walked around a corner and began hobbling towards her. He was stooped over low, and walked very slowly to stand a few metres away from her.

Nayla was more than ready for a fight.

"Let me go," she said. "If you don't let me go, I will kill anything I see."

The voice began to laugh again, but it was not coming from the old man.

"You can not kill me," the voice said. "I am already dead. I am the darkness that rules over this mountain and the forest around it, and I am looking to take over more. I need some helpers."

"Well I will not help," Nayla said. "Never."

"You will, my dear, you will," the voice said. The old man was staring at Nayla with one good eye. The other eye was closed.

"You have been taken over by darkness before, and you will be taken over again," the voice said. "Do you know how to protect yourself against the evil forces? Have you been shown that yet?"

Nayla didn't respond.

"You were supposed to be on a nice little quest, weren't you? You and that other boy? Little did you know, the golden bird that would have carried you home to safety is now owned by me. And soon I will own you too."

"No," Nayla said. "No."

Nayla felt a fear, but beneath her fear was an indomitable will that knew she had more power than whatever was speaking.

"We will see," the voice said. "Attack her."

The old man dropped his walking stick, stood up straight, and charged at Nayla. Nayla saw him reach for a knife in his waistline, and before he could pull out the knife, she stepped off to the side and kicked him straight on the chin.

The man's body went stiff, and he keeled over to land face-first on the floor.

"Where is your fear?" the dark voice said. "You must have some."

"I have some, but I am learning to embrace it," Nayla said. "If you don't let me go, I promise that I will find a way to destroy you."

"You can not," the voice replied. "You should run. They are coming."

Nayla heard something coming from around the corner, in the distance. It sounded like the footsteps of a hundred men, but the footsteps seemed to rattle the walls around her, and the ground beneath her feet began to shake.

"Run!" said the voice.

Nayla knew that the voice around her was trying to make her afraid. Fear told her to run. When she embraced the fear within her, she felt an instinct to stand her ground.

Around the corner appeared a gang of ghouls, dark spirits with huge eyes, no noses and empty mouths. They all began to scream and run towards her, and Nayla decided she would not run away from them.

As the ghouls rushed towards her, they began to look confused, and they slowed down.

"Where is she?" one of them said. "She was there, just now...she was there."

"She's right there!" the darkness of the mountain screamed. "She's in front of you!"

"Where?" another ghoul said. This second ghoul had a tremendously dopey voice.

The ghouls began to scratch their heads. They were quickly getting bored.

"We were promised a chase," another ghoul said. "You promised us a scared little girl that we could chase away."

"She should be afraid!" the dark voice said. "I can see she has been infected by darkness before. One of my spirits got to her mother and began doing some beautiful work through her."

"Well, this is a load of rubbish," the first ghoul said. "We demand a chase. All of us do. If we don't get a good chase, then we will revolt."

"No you won't," the darkness of the mountain said. "What could you do?"

"We will destroy this mountain," the ghouls said.

"And I will just rebuild it," the darkness said, sounding almost tired and bored at the suggestion. "And then you would have nowhere to go."

As Nayla looked around, she felt a tremendous relief. She did not have to fear another bad thing happening again. She did not have to fear the darkness, and if fear appeared in her – it was fine. As long as she embraced it, it was fine. Her embrace of the fear made it her ally, it gave her even more strength.

She began to walk forward, towards the ghouls, and they began to back away.

"I feel sick," the first ghoul said. "There's something in here making me feel sick."

"Me too," another ghoul said. "We were never promised sickness! Just someone scared that we could chase!"

"She's trying to escape!" the darkness of the mountain said. "Stop her!"

"No," the ghouls said, "no we don't feel very well."

Nayla walked through the group of ghouls that moved out of her way, and as she turned the corner, there was a set of stairs. It led upwards, and Nayla began to run up it.

*

"You can't escape here, you know," the darkness said to her as she ran up the stairs. "There is never any escape."

"Thanks for bringing me here," Nayla said as she moved up the stairs.

"What?"

"Thanks for bringing me here. It's taught me a lot about fear, something that I would have never learnt in a dojo. When I was working for my dad, all my life was fear. The fear was so strong it made me want to fight everything all the time to try to stop something bad happening. Without fear, or if I embrace the fear, I can still fight, but I'm not susceptible to darkness anymore."

"Shut up," the darkness said. "This is not how it was supposed to be. You are mine now, and that's that."

"Oh, I do admire your persistence," Nayla said.

The voice of darkness made a groaning sound, as if it had just tasted something very bad.

Nayla made her way to the top of the stairs, where she stood on a platform.

Below her there was a large, clear lake that looked quite inviting. It was shining slightly.

"What's that?" she said. "It looks much nicer than everything else in here."

"That's...that's nothing," the darkness said.

"That's the heart of the mountain, isn't it?" she said, intuitively. "You are just an imposter that has taken over the surface. That's the real heart of the mountain. Look at how clear it is."

As Nayla looked down, she could hear something sniffling and crying.

She peered down over the edge, and sitting on the side of the lake, was a large man that looked as if he was made of stone. Nayla could not see him too clearly in the darkness around the edge of the lake, but he looked as if he was a piece of the mountain that was able to walk around. He was strongly built, with a head, hands and feet larger than a normal man's, and he was sitting there, crying.

"Enough," the darkness said to Nayla. "Enough. You will have to be dealt with physically, if we cannot reach you spiritually."

Nayla heard more footsteps, footsteps rushing up the stairs behind her and breaths of men panting as they ran.

At the top of the stairs appeared a group of soldiers, dressed in dark red, their faces covered in dark masks, holding sticks and swords and weapons that Nayla had never seen.

"Attack her!" the spirit screamed, and as the men rushed forward, Nayla met them with daggers and kicks. As the men struggled to fit through the narrow archway leading on to the ledge where she stood, Nayla was cutting and slashing and throwing and kicking, until these men began to fall. She would throw each man over the ledge, and down towards the water below.

"No!" the darkness screamed, and soon Nayla was alone again, watching the men splashing into the water.

The lake beneath her shone with a very bright white light for a moment, and the dark voice around her started to groan again.

The man that looked as if he was made of the mountain looked up at her and seemed to smile. He had kind eyes that Nayla knew were safe, and she felt compelled to go down and speak with him.

As Nayla made her way down toward the Mountain Man, she saw him looking at her with optimism.

"Hello!" he called.

Nayla was sliding down a thin ninja rope that she had tied to a jagged piece of the mountain near the platform up high, and she could begin to see more clearly his smiling face.

"That was marvellous, what you did! And don't worry about those men, they feel all better now, now that they are back home."

Nayla reached the ground, and began to approach the Mountain Man.

"Hello, I'm the Mountain Man," the Mountain Man said. "I haven't seen anyone like you for a very long time, it's good to see you, it is very good."

"Thanks," Nayla said, sitting down near him, but not too close.

"Why are you here?" she said.

The Mountain Man's face became sad again.

"I have to stay here. If I leave, I think this darkness will take over her heart. This is my mother, this mountain, and if I leave, the darkness will infect the purest part of her. I was born here, you know, straight out of this water, and I have returned to protect it. I can not leave, not ever."

"Has the darkness tried to chase you away?"

"Yes, but I am too strong. His dark forces can not infiltrate me, and his men are not strong enough to harm me. I keep watch over this lake so that nothing tries to poison her."

Nayla looked around. It was as if there were eyes peering down on them, waiting for the Mountain Man to lose his concentration.

"What could they do to it? If you weren't here what would happen?" Nayla asked.

"They would have dark creatures come down and start to put a spell over it, a spell that would destroy the purity of my mother's heart," the Mountain

Man said. "But I won't let them. If they come close I grab them and I snap them in half, then I feed them to the water, which seems to keep it shining brightly."

"Well the darkness is growing stronger on the surface," Nayla said. "How can we get rid of it completely?"

The darkness spoke out from the walls:

"You can't. I am too powerful. I am a collection of thousands of evil spirits that have joined forces over the years. You can not get rid of me, ever."

"There is one way, I think," the Mountain Man said. "Have you ever heard of Light Beings?"

"Shut up," the darkness said.

"Only once," Nayla said.

"They are the most powerful spirits in the world, enlightened creatures that realised their oneness with everything in nature," the Mountain Man said. "If one came here, I think it would help a great deal."

"Nope," the darkness said from the walls. "None dwell close to me. Those Light Beings are too scared and too afraid to try to tussle with me. I am no ordinary force of darkness. I am all the forces in the world, brought together and multiplied."

The Mountain Man looked disheartened again.

"The way out is through this lake," he said. "If you want to escape, you must swim down until you find the tunnel. Swim through the tunnel and you will emerge behind the mountain. But some of the worst creatures dwell there, to make sure nothing leaves."

"Could you help me, to go and find a Light Being?" Nayla said.

"I can not leave here," the Mountain Man said. "I'm sorry."

Nayla sat and watched the Mountain Man stare into the water, and for a moment, she did not know what to do.

*

As Myasako and Takashi finished climbing out of the chasm in the earth, Myasako hugged Takashi.

"Thank you," Myasako said.

Takashi continued to speak to Myasako without using words, placing his thoughts in Myasako's head.

"Where is Nayla?" he said.

"She was taken," Myasako said out loud. Takashi raised his finger to his mouth to indicate 'quiet'.

"You can speak to me without words, I can hear you well enough," Takashi said silently.

Myasako began to try to communicate with Takashi, just by thinking clearly.

"She was taken, snatched away beneath the swamp," Myasako said.

Takashi nodded.

"We must enter the mountain," Takashi said.

Myasako nodded again. He felt that with Takashi by his side, nothing would be able to harm him.

"Where is my father?" Myasako said.

"Praying," Takashi said. "He can not reach us through the darkness that surrounds this place. We must continue alone."

The two ninjas looked up at the mountain which was now close, and together they began to glide, towards the base of the mountain, to try to find Nayla.

*

Behind the base of the mountain, Nayla emerged out of the ground. She was wet from swimming down through the lake, and as soon as she emerged she was attacked. All she could sense were gnashing teeth flying in towards her from the trees, and her instincts told her to duck and slash. There was a strange screaming noise as each set of gnashing teeth swooped in on her, and they made slight yelps as they were slashed in half by her daggers and dropped to the ground.

Nayla looked around her. She sensed something else was going to happen, and that same feeling of something wrapping around her leg emerged beneath her. This time, without the hindrance of any swamp, she cut and stabbed and sliced any tendril or grasping vine that came near her, until she was left well alone, in the darkness. She stood up straight, then began to run around the mountain, to see if she could find Myasako.

Independence

*Life's challenges help you to forge an
independent spirit.*

Chapter 9 - Ninja Skills

When Martin and the Garganfan had finished sparring in the forest, Martin was lying on his back with his arms sprawled out, struggling for breath.

"That was hard," Martin said.

"Interesting isn't it, how much slower and less able you become when you are tired? It happens with everyone." The Garganfan was sitting nearby, with his legs crossed. Nerris and Amanda were sitting down too.

"Yes," Martin said. "And all that grappling, when you had me on the ground – I didn't know what to do."

"It's a work in progress," the Garganfan said, "and a work that never ends. If you ever think you have reached a point where you know everything there is to know about fighting, you are most likely wrong."

"Let's do it again," Martin said after a few minutes had passed. "I want to do it again."

"No," the Garganfan said. "No, we do not want to over-train you. If we do too much today, you will be too fatigued to train again soon. Let us choose consistency over intensity. You have to slowly build your skills."

"Well what can I improve on for next time?" Martin said.

"Calmness," the Garganfan said. "Controlled aggression can be useful in a fight, but panic and struggle are not. When you were on the ground, trying to get free, you exhausted yourself because you had no real leverage, you were just squirming around like a trapped insect because you were starting to panic..."

"I didn't know what else to do," Martin said.

"And you will learn," the Garganfan said, "and you will learn much faster if you can remain calm in those uncomfortable situations. If your body is tense all the time, you become like a hard plank of wood – it might be strong, but it can splinter and break. If you are more relaxed and poised, you become like a living whip, hard to catch and hard to break."

"Okay," Martin said.

"I'm sure Kuyasaki told you something similar in Japan," the Garganfan said.

"He taught me to not expect instant results all the time," Martin said, "and to not compare myself to other people."

"He was teaching you to become free from yourself," the Garganfan said. "If you can train without an insecure sense of self, if you can just train and allow your training to flow, not taking it too personally, this is the quickest route to learning, and also enjoying the process."

"Yes, that was another thing," Martin said. "He taught me to enjoy the process as much as possible."

"Okay," the Garganfan said, standing up. "Amanda, now it's your turn."

"No thanks," Amanda said. She did not want to get squashed on the ground like Martin had just been.

"Let's just do some basics, some easy stuff," the Garganfan said. "A human being who can defend itself is a very powerful creature indeed. Come on, just a few minutes. I did not hurt Martin. I will not hurt you."

Amanda looked at Martin. He was looking at her with encouragement. "Okay," Amanda said, standing up. "But don't squash me."

*

"You seem different to when we first met you," Martin said to the Garganfan. Nerris and Amanda were walking just behind them, back to where they had entered the forest that day.

"Yes, I feel different," the Garganfan said. "Ever since this stone has been in my chest, it's as if I have a full heart again. I'm at ease. Before, all I could think about was fighting, and I was built to either defend the innocent or teach creatures how to fight. That is still my purpose, but I feel like I have much more depth now, as if it is not such a burden to be awake, and I can enjoy the forest even if there is no violence taking place."

"Have you ever heard about this happening to a Garganfan before?" Nerris asked. She hadn't been speaking much for the past few hours, just observing everything.

"There was a tale about a Garganfan, the first of our kind who had a heart brighter than all the rest. But I didn't hear about it having anything to do with a stone."

Nerris didn't say anything back. She looked deep in thought.

"Do you feel stronger with the stone?" Martin said.

"Yes, I do. Not just stronger, but more sensitive, more connected, more able to be in communion with the whole forest. I can sense things much more easily, and I can almost tell what is going to happen before it happens."

The Garganfan held out his hand over Martin's head, and a small twig fell into his hand.

"You see?" the Garganfan said. "And these powers seem to be getting stronger all the time."

Sensitivity

When the mind is liberated from negative impressions, true perception is possible.

Chapter 10 - Emergence

As Nayla ran around the base of the dark mountain, she could hear something calling her from inside the mountain's core.

"The Mountain Man needs your help," the darkness's voice was saying. "I have finally captured him. He needs your help."

Nayla had images in her mind of the Mountain Man trapped in a cage, being prodded with sharp swords while dark creatures cast evil spells over the lake at the heart of the mountain.

She stopped for a moment.

"He needs you," the voice said. Nayla was trying to resist the voice. It couldn't be true. It must be lying to draw me back in, she told herself.

"Nayla!" she heard another voice hiss. It was Myasako, followed closely by Takashi.

Nayla could not see far, but just behind them there seemed to be a strange-looking lump of a creature lying on the ground that Takashi had slain.

"Are you okay?" Myasako said.

"Yes, I'm fine," she said. "But this darkness is getting out of control. We have to stop it."

"How?" Myasako said. "Were you inside?"

"Yes, I was. There's a creature in there called the Mountain Man, sitting by the heart of the mountain, keeping watch over it. He says he cannot leave, but I have a feeling he would be able to help us a great deal."

Myasako cast his mind back to his book at home.

"Is it a man made of stone?" he said.

"Yes," Nayla said.

"Is he warm and friendly but strong and protective?"

"Yes."

"Was he sitting by a pool of water, saying it gave birth to him?"

"Yes!"

"I have an idea," Myasako said. "I know what we can do."

*

Kuyasaki was alone in his room. He had left the mountain where he had prayed to his old master, and now he was wrestling with his feelings. His heart was telling him to stay put, but his fatherly instinct was to run through the entire forest in a desperate attempt to find Myasako.

And then something appeared in front of him. Kuyasaki opened his eyes, and sitting before him, was the shining spirit of his old master, Hirozama.

"Master," Kuyasaki bowed forward, and his master said nothing.

"Your boy is fine," Hirozama said. "For now. Takashi is with him, Nayla too."

At that moment, Nayla's mother, Shieng, made her way down the stairs. She had been up worrying about Nayla still being missing.

"Where are they?" Shieng asked Hirozama. She sat down beside Kuyasaki.

"They are at the base of the Akuma Mountain," Hirozama said. "The darkness there has spread, infecting other creatures further out in the forest. It brought your children directly to itself by way of the Golden Bird."

Kuyasaki was silent for a moment.

"Can you bring them back to us?" Kuyasaki said. "I have made a terrible mistake letting them go."

"Don't be so quick to judge yourself," Hirozama said. "Mistakes can turn out to be just the right thing, if we give them time."

"You are a Light Being, master," Kuyasaki said. "You could easily bring all three of them back safely."

"They have their own work to do," Hirozama said. "There is a reason the three of them are there together. They are on a mission."

"To do what?" Shieng said.

"To restore balance, and free one of the most powerful creatures in the forest."

"Which creature?"

"They call him the Mountain Man."

Balance

Maintain your balance within an optimistic mind.

Chapter 11 - The Great Liberation

The Mountain Man was once again sitting alone by the lake, keeping guard of it so that nothing came near it.

"I will keep you safe," he whispered to the water. "They will never cast a spell over you."

The Mountain Man noticed that the water began to shimmer and vibrate. He saw some bubbles rising up to the surface.

The Mountain Man stood up and watched.

A young boy emerged, Japanese, dressed in black, claiming his name was Myasako and that he had a message to deliver.

"What is it?" the Mountain Man asked, slightly confused. "You look a bit like the girl that was here recently."

"I've come to tell you that you need to get out of here. The mountain will soon collapse and release the evil spirit out into the world."

"I'm not leaving, no way!" the Mountain Man said. "No way am I leaving. If I leave then this mountain's heart will become infected. I will not have that happen!"

"But the mountain is soon to die!" Myasako said. "You have to come and at least save yourself."

"Nope. No way," the Mountain Man said. As he said 'no' for the second time, Nayla and Takashi emerged from the water, leaping out and casting thin ninja cables around the feet and arms of the Mountain Man, snatching him away from the ground and into the water.

The Mountain Man became very angry, he was submerged for a moment, but was far too strong to be dragged for long, and as soon as he hit the water he tried to climb back out again.

But as he clambered back onto the surface, the water had already covered his entire body, and he felt something changing inside him.

"What's happening, mother?! What's happening?!" the Mountain Man cried. Myasako, Nayla and Takashi were in the water, watching as the Mountain Man began to turn brighter. The water looked like it was eating through him, through his outer layer of skin and turning his body into a beam of light.

"Mother, mother I don't want to die!"

Suddenly the light held within the Mountain Man exploded out of him, and the light went crashing upwards into the roof of the hollow mountain.

The darkness's voice in the walls began to wail and scream.

"Stop! Stop this!" the darkness was screaming. "You are hurting me, son, you are hurting me."

"You are not my mother!" the Mountain Man screamed back, and then the form of the Mountain Man exploded, and the entire mountain was filled with light. Every dark creature and spirit hidden in the walls of the mountain began to pour out from their dark, unseen crevices, and they began to sprint towards the water.

The three ninjas jumped out of the way, and they saw every creature run past them, fleeing, trying to escape through the lake, but being dissolved into the water, making it even more pure and clear.

Myasako and Nayla watched as the mountain became completely cleansed of darkness, and the scurrying, crying, falling noises of spirits and creatures began to calm down.

A large piece of dark rock fell from the top of the mountain, and landed straight in the water with a splash, covering the surroundings in this pure, clean water that looked as if it was sparkling.

The Mountain Man was gone, and the three ninjas stood there, feeling as if they had never stood in such a pure place in all their lives.

*

The three ninjas were now standing outside the mountain again, and the forest looked completely different. It was no longer a dark fearful place, but a place that was regenerating by the minute. A great weight had been lifted.

They heard a squawk, a flapping, and the black bird appeared and landed on a branch nearby them. Its feathers looked much cleaner than before.

"Done it! Done it you have!" it said. "A Light Being must have come, didn't see it, didn't see it, no. Where was it? Where was the Light Being?"

"I think we created one," Nayla said. "Where did he go?"

They all felt that they were being watched again, this time by something very benevolent. They turned around and could see a pair of eyes staring at them from the walls of the mountain. The eyes blinked, and out of the mountain stepped a man, the Mountain Man, who now looked even stronger than before.

"I must thank you," the Mountain Man said. His voice was now slower and deeper. "You helped me to realise what I truly am, an immortal of this forest, and you allowed me to save my mother."

The Mountain Man embraced all three ninjas,

squashing them ever so slightly in his arms. All three ninjas felt an overwhelming sense of love flow though their bodies, and the black bird flew and landed on the Mountain Man's shoulder.

"Light Being, Light Being. This is a Light Being!" the bird squawked.

The Mountain Man released the ninjas and stood back.

Myasako watched the bird on his shoulder seem to be injected with power and light. Its body began to change shape, and it was slowly turning into a small, glowing eagle.

"This mountain is my mother, as are all the mountains in the world," the Mountain Man said. "I was sure that I was born here, but now I know that is not true. I was born in a faraway place, in a mountain beside a lake full of bears and fish. But this mountain is still my mother. All of the mountains are one, and from their hearts they produce wonderful things."

"Are there more like you?" Myasako said. "I've read about you, in a book about mythical creatures in a forest far from here."

"It is all the same forest, in truth," the Mountain Man said, "but I do not know if there are more of my kind. I have never met one."

Takashi was still looking around, checking for possible dangers where there were none.

"Where do you live?" the Mountain Man said. "You are surely ready to get back home."

"We live just beyond the Seishin Mountain," Myasako said.

The bird on the Mountain Man's shoulder was now a complete, beautiful eagle with powerful wings and claws. It had become silent.

"All three of you can dive into what used to be the swamp of deceit, the swamp you landed in when you were brought to this place. Request the Seishin Mountain, and you will be taken there."

"Thank you," Myasako said.

"But travel together," the Mountain Man added. "Jump in all three of you, at the same time. You must combine your strength to travel safely."

"Okay, thanks again," Myasako said. "Let's go then."

As Myasako and Takashi bowed and turned to leave, Nayla stood there. She wasn't sure if she really wanted to go home.

"Will we see you again?" she said.

"I'm sure of it," the Mountain Man said. "When the time is right."

Nayla bowed, turned, and the three ninjas made their way to the swamp of deceit, which was now a shining blue pool of light.

*

"How did you know?" Nayla asked as they stood over the blue pool of light. "How did you know that would work?"

"I wasn't sure," Myasako said. "But in that book I told you about, there was a part about the Mountain Man being secretly afraid of the water within any mountain, because he believed it might kill him. The author suspected the water had the power to free the Mountain Man from birth and death, turning him into an immortal who could take a physical form or no form at all. That's what he is now. A Light Being."

Takashi looked down at the water.

"This is not normal transmission water," Takashi said. "I have never seen water this blue. I do not trust it. I suggest we make it home on foot."

"How long will that take?" Myasako said. He was low on energy.

"Hours. But I do not trust this water."

Nayla looked down into the shining pool.

"I want to try it. The Mountain Man said we just have to make our request. We request the Seishin Mountain," she said.

"Nayla, no," Takashi said. "We are not familiar with this kind of water. It looks tremendously powerful."

"I've had enough of being told what to do," Nayla said. "My father ordered me around all of my life, and I want to be free from it." She was now on a high from defeating the darkness of the mountain, and something inside her did not want the adventure to end.

She felt like she was strong enough to do anything.

"I'm trying it," she said.

"Nayla, no!" Takashi said.

Nayla leapt and jumped into the water, and as she made a splash, she disappeared, and the water flashed with light.

Transcendence

To transcend one thing,
you must cease your resistance against it.

Chapter 12 - The Interceptors

The Interceptors were a strange group of creatures. They looked like rats, as tall as small children, and they were always walking on their hind legs. They wore clothes because they were embarrassed of being naked like all the other animals. They found nakedness to be the equivalent of savagery. Wearing clothes was a sign that they had evolved beyond the base level of existence, and now they were beginning to thrive.

"We have one!" one of them said. "A big one." A group of Interceptors were in their main underground meeting room, where they were watching a small puddle of water in the middle of the ground, which was shining with a very slight blue light.

"It's a girl, alone, travelling to a mountain," one of them said. This one was sitting with its eyes closed, and it had a cable connected from its ear to the puddle of water.

"Alone? Are you sure?" another Interceptor said. Their noses began to twitch more furiously than normal.

"Yes, maybe not for long."

"Catch it, draw it in!" the head Interceptor cried out. This Interceptor was taller, and wore a small green jacket with a badge on the chest.

An Interceptor holding a small fishing line appeared, and threw one end of the line down into the water, and waited. There was a silence as all of the Interceptors waited, all holding their breath, and then the fishing Interceptor began to struggle.

"Got it! Got it!" the Interceptor yelled. "Help! Help!"

The Interceptor was nearly dragged down into the puddle beneath them, but a group of Interceptors rallied behind him, grabbed him by the waist and began to pull him backwards.

"I'm reeling it in!" the fishing Interceptor yelled.

"Keep going."

The struggle continued for minutes, something on the other end of their line was extremely strong, but caught up and trapped. The Interceptors kept pulling, yelling 'heave!' every second, and with one final pull, a girl emerged out of the puddle of water, and fell onto the ground.

She was exhausted, tangled in their fishing line but still ready to fight. She stood up, drew out daggers and instantly began to attack the Interceptors around her.

"Run!" the head Interceptor yelled, and as some Interceptors were caught by blades and cut, they were so rapid that all managed to escape and squeeze into little holes in the walls that led to tunnels. The holes were too small for Nayla to squeeze through.

The room was empty. Nayla knew she was underground somewhere. She jumped back into the puddle of water, but now instead of being an endless depth of liquid energy, it was shallow. Her feet hit the bottom and the water came up to her ankles.

"Where am I!?" she yelled. "Let me go! I requested the Seishin Mountain!"

There were giggles and sniggers coming from the walls.

"We live just below the mountain," the head Interceptor said. "You should never travel alone through the lakes and rivers, you know."

Nayla looked for other ways of escape. She was surrounded by dirt walls and little holes with sniffs and sniggers coming out of them.

"Why am I here?" she called out.

"We catch whatever we can. Usually we just get injured, fallen birds that have dropped into the water by accident, and have been carried towards us by mistake. We've never had a creature like you before."

"But why? Why am I here?" Nayla asked again.

More sniggers emerged.

"We like to collect things," the head Interceptor said. "We like to keep things alive, and they keep us alive."

"What do you mean?" Nayla said.

"You'll see," the Interceptor said. "You'll see soon enough."

*

For weeks, the Garganfan refused to take Martin anywhere further in the forest. All they did was train, again and again, often very similar drills and techniques, until the Garganfan began to grow satisfied that Martin was able to defend himself reasonably well.

"You have made very good progress," the Garganfan said.

This time he and Martin were alone. Nerris and Amanda were back at the house. Nerris had recently become obsessed over a new invention that she refused to speak about.

"Thanks," Martin said. "I've enjoyed it. I feel more powerful, stronger and more confident in my body."

"That comes from consistency, and good training," the Garganfan said.

"I'm going to have to go back to school soon," Martin said. "My holidays are almost over. I'll be moving back home, away from Nerris. I won't be able to come into the forest and stay for so long, but my house is still close to the forest. It's just at a different spot."

The Garganfan nodded.

"You must do what you must do," he said.

There was a silence, a tremendous silence where Martin wasn't thinking about anything at all.

"Would you like to meet one of my most favourite creatures?" the Garganfan said. "Your mother has told me it is okay for you to meet this one."

"Yes!" Martin said, springing up to his feet. "Where is it? What is it?"

"Come, I'll show you," the Garganfan said.

Friendship

True friends help each other to become greater beings in the world.

Chapter 13 - The Suppression

When Martin was back at school, he had a terrible feeling as if his freedom was being stolen from him.

"Where have you been?" his friend Harry said from beside him before the class started. "What have you been up to for the past few weeks? I couldn't get through to you, you weren't at home..."

"Sorry," Martin said. "I...I had to go away."

"To do what? Go on holiday?" Harry asked.

"Kind of," Martin said. "Kind of."

"Okay, class!" Their teacher walked in holding a pile of papers. Her name was Miss Neswith, a flowery teacher who always wore flowery dresses. The children liked her because she was kind, but they did not fear her like some of the other teachers.

"So it's your first day back. Are you all excited?"

There was silence in the class.

"I thought today we would break into things with something nice and easy. I want each of you to write about what you got up to in the school holidays, and go into detail about your favourite thing you did. Then I'll ask some of you to get up in front of the class and read about your favourite thing from your break from school. How does that sound?"

It staggered Martin that Miss Neswith assumed that the students were happy to be back in the classroom. She handed him a piece of paper, and he began to write.

Forty-five minutes passed. Harry had spent most of his time staring out of the window, chewing his finger. He had written his name, and the title: "What I Did On Holyday."

"Okay!" Miss Neswith suddenly said. It made Martin jump slightly. "Who would like to read first?"

A few children put their hands up. Martin was amazed at this too.

"Harry? Harry would you like to read what you've written for us?"

The whole class looked at Harry.

"No thanks, Miss, I'll let someone else have a go."

"Harry," Miss Neswith said more sternly.

"I don't want to be selfish, Miss. Let someone who wants to read have a go. I'm alright just listening."

"Harry Oswald, please, stand up in front of the class and read your favourite thing about your school holidays. Now. I do not want to contact the headmaster."

Although Miss Neswith did not rule the class by fear too often, if she ever had to, she could just mention the headmaster, Mr Ostrich. No one wanted to be anywhere near Mr Ostrich, ever.

"Okay," Harry said, standing up while grabbing his blank piece of paper and walking up to the front of the class.

Martin watched as Harry stood there. Harry was angling his paper away from the teacher so she couldn't see he had not written anything.

Harry cleared his throat.

"I would like to begin by saying," Harry said, "that the school holidays were a wonderful time, for all of us, weren't they? I did many amazing things and..."

"Harry, just read what you've written please," Miss Neswith said.

"Okay, okay," Harry said, "but before I begin..."

"Harry," Miss Neswith barked. "Just read."

"Yes, of course," Harry said, adjusting himself as

he stood, "of course, Miss Neswith."

He cleared his throat again, and began to pretend to read.

"My favourite thing this summer was when I went horseback riding with my aunty Julie. She owns a horse stable out in the country, and she asked me if I would like to come down to spend the day with the horses..."

Martin watched as Harry gave a detailed, in-depth speech about his experience horseback riding out in the country. Martin knew that Harry's only aunt was named Grace, and she owned a hair salon in the centre of town. Martin watched and listened in amazement, for ten minutes, until Harry began to end his speech...

"I felt that I had for the first time seen inside the mind of an animal, and I also conquered my fear of failure. It was a wonderful day."

As he finished, the whole class knew he had made it up, but nearly everyone admired Harry for his spontaneous genius.

"Harry, that was marvellous, absolutely marvellous! I've never known writing like that from you before, may I see your paper? I would like to keep it as a prime example of what a good piece of work should be."

"No, Miss, no, I want to keep it, it's special to me, I'm proud of myself," Harry said, putting his hand on his heart.

Miss Neswith sat back, not wanting to spoil the boy's sense of accomplishment.

"Okay, very well. That's very well done, Harry. Go and take a seat."

Harry walked back towards his chair, with his chin in the air, avoiding any eye contact with anyone in case he began to smile too much.

"So who is next, Martin?" Miss Neswith said, "Martin will you come to the front?"

Martin stood up, walked to the front of the class, faced everyone, and began to read.

"My favourite part of the school holidays was meeting a creature known as the Garganfan," Martin began.

Some of the classmates giggled.

"The Garganfan is often assumed to be a purely mythical creature, but I have recently been to the Oakmound Forest over in Feddleditch where my aunt Nerris lives, which connects to the same forest that sits behind our school. There I met the Garganfan, and he introduced me to another mythical creature that turned out to be real..."

"Martin!" the teacher hissed as more of the class began to laugh. "Is this really what you have written? I wanted a real-life account, not something made up!"

"But this is real," Martin said. "This is what happened."

"Go outside," Miss Neswith said, embarrassed after such a fine piece of work from Harry. "You know better than this. Go outside and wait for the headmaster."

"But don't you want to hear about the Jogglegog?" Martin said.

"Certainly not. We are not writing fiction. Now wait outside, please."

Martin dropped his piece of paper to his side, folded it up neatly and put in in his pocket. He walked outside, and waited without fear, for the headmaster that everyone was afraid of.

*

When a child was called to see the headmaster, usually they would leave the class and visit the headmaster's office. It used to happen regularly, until one child decided they would rather run away than take a yelling from one of the scariest men they had ever seen. A young man named Terrence was reported to have fled the school on his way through the corridors, disappearing into the woods behind the school gates, never to be seen again.

Nowadays the headmaster was called out of his office, to visit the child directly outside of the classroom, where they remained in sight of their teacher through the small window of each classroom door.

Martin was standing there, in view of Miss Neswith who would occasionally dart her eyes toward him. She had already been on the phone, and Martin knew who it was to.

And then Martin heard the footsteps that every child in the school dreaded – heavy footsteps that made the floor shake slightly, and from around the empty corner of the empty corridor ahead of him, a large, top-heavy man with a limp strode straight across the wooden floor towards him.

Martin used to be afraid of this man too, but after the past few weeks spent with the Garganfan, Martin wasn't very scared at all. What would this man do? He had one bad leg, and both of his legs were far too small for the rest of his body. He had a massive stomach, a shirt that was too tight, and oily hair that looked as if it had not been washed for weeks. The only thing that made Martin recoil was the smell.

"Lies? Been making up lies have you, boy?" the

headmaster said as he reached him. His name was Mr Ostrich, but he did not remind Martin of a bird. A monster, perhaps, but not a bird.

"No, sir," Martin said.

"Let me see, let me see what you've been reading out to the class."

Martin took out from his pocket the work he had been doing, and handed it to the man. Martin stepped back slightly. The smell of the man was stinging the back of his throat a little bit.

The man stood and read, and every time he breathed his nostrils seemed to wheeze.

"What's this?" he said, thrusting the paper back at Martin.

"A Garganfan?" his hand trembled. "What's this other creature, a Jogglegog? What on earth is that?"

Martin stared at the headmaster. He noticed that the headmaster's eyes were starting to twitch, something that Martin had never seen happen before.

"What? Answer me, boy, what are you staring at?"

"What's the question, sir?" Martin said.

"The question is...erm...what, what on earth are you doing writing about this sort of thing in class? You know full well it should be kept..."

The headmaster stopped himself from speaking.

"Secret? Were you about to say secret, sir?"

"No, you know I wasn't, no, I mean..."

The headmaster began to fumble over his words.

"You must not go speaking of such things, such made-up things in class," the headmaster said. His tone had become slightly kinder. "You...you mustn't write about such things ever again, is that understood?"

The headmaster began to back away.

"Sir?"

The headmaster turned to walk away, and Martin watched the man hobbling off in a hurry.

Soon Martin was left alone again, and he was sure that as the headmaster turned the corner at the end of the corridor, he began to run.

*

Martin very nearly went back inside the classroom, resigning to the fact that he could not tell the truth about his time in the forest. The strange behaviour of the headmaster was still on his mind. Mr Ostrich wasn't ever one to back away from a student. As

Martin turned to walk towards the classroom door, he saw Miss Neswith busy teaching her class, now focussing away from Martin and his meeting with the headmaster. She had forgotten all about him.

Martin stopped himself from reaching for the door, and he decided he would follow the headmaster instead.

He began to run, very quietly along the corridor, around the corner, and down the flights of stairs towards the headmaster's office. As he ran, he could hear the grunting and stamping in the distance, as the headmaster was still on the move.

Martin could glide with ease now. After having spent so long creeping and running and gliding with the Garganfan in the forest, now the element of stealth was very natural to him, something that seemed to be in his blood.

The shuffling, stamping and grunting got louder, and Martin caught up to the headmaster so that as he reached the bottom of the stairs, he could see the headmaster walking towards his office.

Martin watched from the bottom of the stairwell. Something had shaken the man's mind, and instead of going into his office, the headmaster stepped outside.

He stepped onto a field, it was a field kept far away

from the eyes of classrooms, teachers and children, and the only door to it was in the headmaster's private corridor which Martin was now on.

Martin ran to the door and watched.

He watched as Mr Ostrich marched across the field, towards the metal fencing in the distance.

Martin watched as Mr Ostrich approached the fence, and instead of using any kind of gate, Mr Ostrich dove down into the ground, hands-first. He could dig down as fast as Martin could run, and soon Mr Ostrich was on the other side of the fence, disappearing into the forest.

Martin could either go back to class, or keep track of Mr Ostrich to see where he was going and who he really was. He decided that in the best interests of the school, it was surely his duty to follow after the headmaster, and so Martin ran out of the door, glided across the field, and pursued this strange Mr Ostrich.

Rebellion

Rebellion can come with risk,
but the rebel does not care.

Chapter 14 - The Denwitch

"It's outrageous!" Mr Ostrich yelled. "Absolutely outrageous! He mentioned the Garganfan and the Jogglegog! If he keeps venturing into the forest, especially with that Garganfan by his side, he is sure to find out about me and what I am. You promised. You promised me that I would never be found out."

"Oh, calm down," a strange and sickly voice said. "Just calm down."

Martin was amongst the trees, watching from afar as he spied on Mr Ostrich who was talking to someone that Martin couldn't see.

Mr Ostrich had his back to Martin, and Mr Ostrich was standing, looking slightly shaky on his bad leg, facing someone whose voice made Martin's skin crawl.

"He will not find out about you, don't worry," the voice said. "If he ever does, no one will believe him anyway. And we can always deal with him ourselves."

"I want the boy dealt with now," Mr Ostrich said. "I don't want him interfering in my job or my work or my reputation. You know what the risks are. If you aren't seen as a human in their world, you are seen as more of an object. They'll either hunt me down or make me dig for hours on building sites or something like that. We have to deal with him right now."

"You must calm down," the sickly voice said. "You know I can't stand you being panicked for too long."

Mr Ostrich took a breath.

The sickly voice began to sniff the air.

"Were you followed here?"

"No."

"Are you sure?"

Mr Ostrich looked behind him, and Martin fully hid himself behind a tree.

"Why do you ask?" Mr Ostrich said.

"I smell something, something different, something young and fresh and inquisitive. Something slightly defiant."

Martin heard a shuffling as something in front of Mr Ostrich began to move.

Martin began to creep away.

"There it is! Through the trees!" the voice said. "Oooh it's a boy!"

Martin suddenly felt his feet leave the ground, and he was turned upside-down, held in the air as he struggled, and he was brought close to where Mr Ostrich was.

"That's him, that's the one!" Mr Ostrich said.

As Martin was turned around, he saw Mr Ostrich looking at him with fury, fists clenched, and sitting in front of Mr Ostrich sat a creature that Martin recognised from Nerris's book, Mythical Creatures Of The Forest. It was a red-skinned, claw-handed witch dressed in black, who had a very slight smile on her face.

*

"What are you going to do with him?" Mr Ostrich said. They had been staring at Martin for a while as he hung upside-down in the air.

"Well he's a spy," the Denwitch said. "I'm quite fond of spies. There are some other Denwitches I would like to spy on, but they can see me coming a mile away. If I masked this one's scent, perhaps he would be quite effective."

"Why are you out here, Mr Ostrich?" Martin said. He was still being held upside-down and all the blood was collecting in his head.

Mr Ostrich said nothing.

"Did you never have your suspicions?" the Denwitch said to Martin. Her hands looked like the feet of eagles, but blacker, and larger. They occasionally would tap the ground, and point towards Martin to keep him suspended.

For some reason, and without him noticing, Martin was quickly forgetting that he recognised the Denwitch from the book at Nerris's house. It was if all the information he had about her in his mind was leaking out without him seeing.

"Well what are you? What is he?" Martin said with a certain fearlessness.

"I'm a Denwitch. He's my son," the Denwitch said.

"Well so what?" Martin said. "What's so bad about that?"

"Do you know about the last person found to be the son of a witch?" the Denwitch said. "It was hundreds of years ago, before we all had to go into hiding. Denwitches have powers, but our sons often do not. Usually they have one strange and fairly useless ability, such as the ability to dig faster than a fox."

Mr Ostrich looked at the ground, embarrassed.

"What about your daughters?" Martin said.

"Our daughters are so powerful that they are

dangerous. We prefer to have sons. They are far easier to control."

"Well what's the problem?" Martin said. "I'm feeling bad, by the way, my head is so full of blood."

The Denwitch laid him on his side very slowly, but Martin still couldn't move.

"I'm not gonna tell anyone, I don't care about all this," Martin continued. The blood started to move back into his body. "But even if anyone found out about Mr Ostrich – couldn't you just use your powers to protect him?"

"No," the Denwitch said. "Our powers are limited, and to spend our energy trying to protect our sons all the time, all day and all night, leads us to exhaustion and an untimely death. Denwitches have tried it, only to leave their sons still vulnerable and at the mercy of witch hunters."

"No one cares about witches anymore," Martin said. "No one even believes in them."

"Really?" the Denwitch said. "Are you sure?"

"Yes. No one believed me in the class anyway, Mr Ostrich. They all thought I was either joking or mad."

Mr Ostrich looked like he was settled slightly.

"Very well, you make a good case," the Denwitch said. "So you promise that you will never, ever, mention this to anyone, never mention that your headmaster is the son of a witch?"

"I promise," Martin said. He was growing frustrated that he was not allowed to move.

"Let me move at least a bit, please," Martin said.

The grip around him loosened, very slightly. He could not sit up.

"Are you satisfied, Ozzy?" she said to her son.

Mr Ostrich nodded.

Martin chose not to question the name 'Ozzy'.

"Very well, but before you go I need a favour from you," the Denwitch said to Martin. "You were so good at creeping that I need you to creep up on someone else. You need to take something from somewhere and bring it back to me. Then I will let you go forever. I just need one thing."

"Well what is it?" Martin said. "You don't mean stealing, do you?"

"Of course not," the Denwitch said, smiling. "No, it's more of a retrieval than anything else."

Martin looked at Mr Ostrich, who was already walking off back to the school. Martin didn't seem to have a choice at the moment.

"Well what is it?" he said

"I can show you," the Denwitch said. "But you must handle it with care."

The Denwitch disappeared into a hole in the ground that was covered in leaves. She re-emerged, climbing out, holding a glowing orb of light that looked as if it was made of glass.

"This is my orb of power," she said. "It's what allows me to be able to hold you in place, like I'm doing now. I can do little tricks and mind-masks and all sorts of things, but it's not enough. I want more, and there's another Denwitch not too far from here who has an orb as well. It's like this one, but it's green, and she...she stole it from me and I want it back."

Martin looked into the glowing orb, and felt a sense of pure power flowing into him, ever so slightly.

"With another orb I will be twice as powerful," the Denwitch said. "I will be able to put more powerful spells on people, hex people, all kinds of things. Denwitches have always been known as the lesser witch. It has been said that we do not have pure enough minds to be blessed with more powers. Everyone talks about the powerful witches being more like angels, but that's rubbish. The powerful

141

witches I've met were horrible, nasty people who always wanted to keep us Denwitches down in the dirt. I'm just trying to do my bit for my own species."

Martin could feel the grip around him loosening.

"Are you loosening that on purpose?" Martin said.

The Denwitch yawned. She looked far more tired than a few minutes ago.

"No, just shut up and do this for me will you? Then I will let you go and be free."

"But you will have to let me go for me to creep up and get this for you, won't you?" Martin said.

"Yes," the Denwitch said.

"Let me go then."

"Will you do it?" the Denwitch said "Will you stea...I mean will you retrieve the green orb for me?"

"Well, what will happen if I don't?" Martin said.

"I'll cut you up into pieces with my claws while I still have a grip over you," she said.

She lunged at him with a single sharp claw ready to slice at his throat.

"Okay. Of course, of course I will," Martin said quickly. Fear ran through him. Martin didn't usually like to tell lies, they had a way of always turning around to bite him in the back at some point, but he didn't know what else to do.

"Okay," the Denwitch said. She snapped her claws together and Martin was free. He could move around exactly as he wanted. The Denwitch yawned and lay on her side on an old fallen tree stump.

"Your scent is masked, so you will be undetectable by a Denwitch," she said, closing her eyes. "Bring it back to me, the orb, I just need to lie down for a bit. It took a lot of energy to control you there."

"Okay," Martin said. As the Denwitch drifted off to sleep, Martin felt very confused.

The Denwitch had no hold over him anymore. He didn't have to do anything.

He crept away from the Denwitch, as silently as he could move. When he was far enough away, he ran back towards the school.

As Martin ran away from the Denwitch, he reached the fencing where Mr Ostrich had still left a tunnel in the ground to crawl through. Suddenly Martin remembered something from the book at Nerris's house, the one rule of dealing with Denwitches:

If you ever deal with a Denwitch, know that she will only truly ever hold one power over you – your own words. If you promise her something or agree to something, you will never be free until you do it.

Martin had a sinking feeling in his chest. Why hadn't he remembered this before? Perhaps it was from the fear of being cut up into small pieces. As he went to crawl down through the tunnel in the ground, he realised he couldn't. There seemed to be a barrier, an invisible barrier stopping him from leaving the forest. More knowledge of the Denwitch began to trickle into his mind, as if it had been kept apart from him for a while and was trying to get back in. Martin stood and turned to face the forest, realising that now he had to keep his word and steal for the Denwitch, or else he would never be free.

*

Martin sat for a while in the forest and tried to remember every word he had read about Denwitches in Nerris's book. He remembered the final line that had been written about them:

The only way to break the bond between the Denwitch and your word, is to kill the Denwitch you made the promise to.

Martin wasn't sure if he could kill the Denwitch he had just met. Not only were those claws sharp and dangerous, he felt like this was all his fault for wondering into the forest alone...again.

Martin stood up, and he realised that the Denwitch had not told him where the green orb was located. If he was going to consider doing this to free himself, he would have to go back and ask her where it was.

As he walked back through the trees, he could hear the Denwitch snoring. Martin walked slowly up to her, and pushed her on the shoulder.

"Excuse me, you didn't tell me where to go," Martin said. "Excuse me...Mrs Denwitch."

The Denwitch snorted and rolled on to her side, but she was not waking up. Martin then remembered that Denwitches don't nap. They sleep for days and stay awake for only one.

As Martin looked down at the red skin and the limp claws, he wondered if he would be able to do something to end this hold she now had over him. He thought of choking her with his legs for a moment, and then the Garganfan appeared.

"That's a fine mess you're now in, isn't it?" the Garganfan said. He was up in the trees, looking down.

Martin looked up at him.

"You knew? You knew I was here?"

"A bird just told me what has been happening. I was quite far away when it happened, I came as soon as I could."

"I told her I would do something, steal something," Martin said.

"Did you?" the Garganfan said. "Did you say that you would steal something?"

Martin cast his mind back.

"Well, actually no, she nearly said steal, but she actually said retrieve."

"Retrieve what?"

"A green orb."

"Well that's not hers," the Garganfan said. "That would be stealing, not retrieving."

The Garganfan jumped down from the trees, picked up the blue orb of the Denwitch, and smashed it into the ground.

The Denwitch lurched awake and drew a breath in with such foulness and harshness that Martin had to cover his ears.

She clutched at her chest, swiped at Martin with her claws, and Martin leaned back and moved away.

The Denwitch fell to her knees.

"You know the oath you made when you sought refuge here," the Garganfan said to her. She was clutching at his feet.

"You know the oath you made with the Earthman. You promised that you would never deceive any creature in the forest, and you have tried to deceive this young boy. I suspect you even placed a very subtle mask over his mind so that he would not remember any of the details he had read about you and how you gain a hold of people."

Martin did notice that his mind felt more muddy than normal.

The Denwitch was trying to plead with the Garganfan but she could not speak. The blue orb's liquid was filtering into the ground through the leaves on the forest floor.

Martin looked at the Garganfan's eyes. They were completely cold. The stone was in his chest, but he seemed to have a fury within him that hated to see treachery amongst his own kind.

"You must now make a new deal," the Garganfan said. "The Earthman is not far away from passing on, you know, so I must take you to him. Let's go."

The Garganfan hoisted a gasping and thrashing Denwitch on to his shoulders, and he turned to

Martin. He changed his tone, and became light and friendly again.

"I think it's time you met the Earthman," the Garganfan said.

Your Word

Let your words reflect your most noble intentions.

Chapter 15 - The Earthman

They walked for quite a while.

"The school will be wondering where I am," Martin said as he followed the Garganfan. The Denwitch was still being held over the Garganfan's shoulder, silently screaming at the air for an ounce of breath. She kept clutching at her throat.

"Don't worry about them," the Garganfan said. "I'm sure that Mr Ostrich will reassure everyone that you are just fine."

"So we are going to meet the Earthman?" Martin said. "That was one of the main creatures in the book that I was reading at Nerris's house. They are born straight out of the ground, aren't they?"

"Yes," the Garganfan said. "And sometimes they are a result of human evolution. This Earthman, for instance, was the author of that book of research you are describing. As he wrote the book, he began to turn into an Earthman himself. That was many years ago, and he is now ready to pass on."

They approached a very large, wide and low-reaching willow tree, whose branches had to be parted for the Garganfan to walk through. Martin followed after, and soon he, the Garganfan and the suffocating Denwitch were in a small, shaded haven, surrounded by the protection of the willow.

At the base of the trunk of the ancient tree, there sat a large figure of an Earthman.

He had no hair, he was larger and more muscular than a normal man, and he seemed to have a third eye in his forehead.

There was a strong silence emanating from him.

The Garganfan approached the Earthman, who stared at all three of them. When Martin met his gaze, he saw the Earthman smile slightly, and something seemed to wake up inside of him, an extra power he never knew he had.

"This one broke the rules," the Garganfan said, laying the writhing Denwitch down on the ground. "She tried to trick this young boy into committing theft. This is Martin, Martin this is the Earthman."

Martin nodded at the Earthman. He didn't feel like disturbing the quietness that was emanating from this shining creature. The Earthman nodded back. He was clearly weak at this stage, and not able to say a great deal.

His eyes blinked very slowly.

The Earthman clicked his fingers, and the Denwitch regained her breath and stopped thrashing around. She stood to her feet quickly.

"I never! I never lied! The boy knew full well what he was agreeing to!"

"You asked him to retrieve, not steal," the Garganfan said. "You knew full well that any lying or theft on your part would mean your powers would be revoked."

"This isn't fair," the Denwitch said. "I haven't done anything wrong."

"Such a dishonest creature," the Garganfan said, disappointedly.

"Come on, let's go," the Garganfan said to Martin, gesturing for Martin to walk out of the willow.

"Can't we stay?" Martin whispered. "Can't I speak more to him? I want to say thanks for the book."

The Garganfan stopped.

"Okay, but not yet. Wait until he's done speaking with the Denwitch. Let's wait outside." The Garganfan led Martin out of the willow branches, and they sat outside, waiting for the Denwitch to emerge.

*

"What if she tries to hurt him?" Martin whispered. He and the Garganfan were sitting in the most beautiful part of the forest Martin had ever seen. It looked as if the trees were shining with golden light.

"Hurt him with what? Her claws?" the Garganfan said.

Martin nodded.

"Don't worry. He may be close to death, but he is still very powerful. Some say he's more powerful than he's ever been because the purity of the forest is shining through his weakened physical form."

The two companions heard a rustling, and from behind them emerged the Denwitch. Her skin was not so red, and her hands were no longer claws. They looked like human hands.

"Gentlemen," she acknowledged the two, nodding, and wandered off into the forest with an innocence that reminded Martin of Jacobson Muldridge when he was demonstralised by Nerris.

"Let's go back in," the Garganfan said.

The two walked back in through the branches, and Martin walked up to the Earthman.

"I...I just wanted to say thanks for writing that book. I didn't realise you were turning into an Earthman as you were writing it. I've only got one half of your diary as well, and I don't know where I can find the second part."

The Earthman reached behind him and pulled out a book that seemed to look remarkably clean and white. He opened the book to near the end, and he began to write something.

Martin looked at the Garganfan, who was saying nothing. The stone in his heart seemed to be shifting from blue to green.

The Earthman finished writing after a while, and he handed the book to Martin.

"Now my memoirs are complete," the Earthman said in a deep voice. "You may undergo changes yourself. Do not fear them. The forest is more powerful than you could imagine."

The Garganfan dropped to his knees, a few feet away from the Earthman.

Martin wasn't sure what was happening, but he watched as the Earthman closed his eyes, and his breathing began to move very slowly.

Martin felt like falling to his knees too. He did, and with a final breath inwards, the Earthman exhaled, relaxed, and disappeared from view, as if he had dissolved back into the willow behind him.

Death

For some, death does not exist.
To them, death is like simply shedding clothes.

Chapter 16 - Entrapment

Nayla was still trapped in an underground cave of the Interceptors. She could hear them preparing something in their tunnels through the holes that she could not squeeze through.

She took out her daggers and began to stab at the walls to make the holes bigger.

"I wouldn't do that if I were you!" came a sniggering voice from the walls. "It might collapse your little enclosure, leaving you trapped under the weight of an entire mountain."

As Nayla continued to dig away, not listening to the advice, the ceiling above her made a strange cracking noise. She stopped immediately, and a large crack formed just above her head.

"Told you," one of the Interceptors said. "Just hold on. We will be moving you to another location soon enough."

Nayla heard a squeaking sound, and then a sound of a machine being turned on. She could feel a slight breeze being blown in through one of the holes in the walls down by her feet. The room began to smell of something rotten, and as she breathed, her vision became blurry.

She lost her balance and suddenly she was on her

side, on the ground, not able to stand up, and just as she was losing consciousness, she could see the Interceptors all crawling back towards her through their holes in the walls, picking up her body, and preparing to move her to somewhere else.

*

When Nayla woke up she was tied to a wall, in a much larger room. Interceptors were scurrying around everywhere and there was a large machine in the middle of the room with a few cables running out of it, with some of the Interceptors beginning to drag the cables towards Nayla.

One of them spotted her.

"Awake! It's awake!" the Interceptor screamed.

"It's awake too early!" another one screamed, and Nayla watched as a mass panic flooded through all of the Interceptors. They had never dealt with something this large before, with such resilience, and Nayla began to feel an excitement bubbling up within her.

Her hands and feet were tied to the wall, but her hands and fingers were flexible enough to reach down to touch her own wrists, where she began to untie herself.

The Interceptors were so panicked they did not notice what she was doing, and with her extreme finger strength, Nayla soon had untied the ropes from around her wrists, and her hands were free.

She reached for her daggers, which were not by her side.

She untied her ankles from the wall, fell down to the ground, and saw at the far side of the room, the head of the Interceptors was staring at her with a look of terror on its face.

"Run! It's free!" the head Interceptor yelled.

This time Nayla could grab Interceptors who were scurrying around her.

They only had one way out, through a tunnel behind where she stood, and although some managed to scurry past her, many of them were trapped.

"It will destroy us all!" the head Interceptor said. "Attack it!"

Some of the Interceptors jumped up and tried to bite at her face, but Nayla was far too fast and began to strike, grab and throw any Interceptor who was near her. She became furious, she punched and kicked through the machine with the cables sticking out of it in the middle of the room, and she went straight for the head Interceptor.

"Protect me! I must be protected!" it yelled.

Now it was chaos, and no one was willing to sacrifice themselves for the leader. Nayla ran across to the head Interceptor, picked him up, and demanded to be set free.

"Okay! Okay!" the head Interceptor said. It was a large, fearful rat with no good ideas left.

"And my weapons?" Nayla said. "Where are they?"

"We'll get them, we will get them for you," the Interceptor said. Nayla was holding up the head Interceptor like a baby, but ready to pull his limbs off his body.

"Get the weapons! Get the weapons!" it shouted out.

Some Interceptors appeared, carrying Nayla's daggers and nunchuks.

"Now. The way out?" Nayla said, picking up her weapons with one hand, and securing them at her waist.

"There's no easy way out," the head Interceptor said. "We Interceptors have lived under the mountain for hundreds of years, and we have never had a good reason to leave. We have everything we need here already."

"What were those cables for, and that machine?"

159

Nayla said. All of the other Interceptors had fled the room. It was now just her and the head Interceptor, and she had him pinned to the floor.

"It was...it was nothing," the head Interceptor said.

Nayla squeezed his neck until he could barely breathe.

"It's our harvester!" the head Interceptor spluttered. "We harvest energy from living things. It sustains us, it keeps us fed. The machine gives the energy out to us in the air, and we use it to survive."

"Do you have other creatures you are harvesting?" she said.

"They've all died. We were praying for a new catch, and then you showed up."

Nayla felt slightly sickened.

"So there's no way out?"

"No," the Interceptor said. "Not unless you go through the water again. But who knows where you might end up?"

Nayla looked around at the dirt walls surrounding her.

"How did you all get here in the first place?" she said.

"A tunnel," the Interceptor said. "A tunnel which has since been sealed to prevent intruders entering."

"Show me where it is," Nayla said. "I need to see it."

Ferocity

Do not let the world dampen your fierceness,
but let your inner wisdom dictate when to use it.

Chapter 17 - The Transition

As Martin and the Garganfan were walking back towards Martin's school, Martin was full of questions. They were both looking rather sombre.

"So, he just died? We just watched him die?" Martin said.

"The Earthman never dies," the Garganfan said. "But he does lose his form after a while. Forms are temporary, but the spirit within them lives on. He was never a man, just the spirit of the forest that could get up and move around for a while."

"Are there any others like him?" Martin said.

"Not around here. He brought up some young Earthchildren in the forest who used to be very much like yourself. Since then they have matured, and some are now taking care of forests overseas."

"When he looked at me I felt very strange, like something shifted inside of me," Martin said.

"He has a way of awakening powers that creatures never knew they had. He may have stirred something within you."

Martin and the Garganfan kept walking back to the edge of the forest where the school was.

"How much longer do you have left at school today?"

"A few hours, I think," Martin said.

"Well come and meet me afterwards," the Garganfan said. "I have something to show you."

Awakening

Do not assume you are finished unlocking all that lies within you.

Chapter 18 - The Great Escape

Nayla was still carrying the head Interceptor in her arms so that it did not run away from her.

"Through here," it said. It was leading her through a series of tunnels that she could barely squeeze through. She was on her stomach, shuffling through the dirt with her knees and elbows.

"Not far to go now," the Interceptor said.

Suddenly Nayla stopped. She had a terrible feeling arise inside her, and she wasn't sure why. She had not been trained to use her intuition by her father, Senzi, but Kuyasaki had been talking about intuition to her since she arrived at his dojo.

Something's not right, she thought, and then Kuyasaki appeared in her mind. He said:

"Intuition will often not match what the thoughts in your head are saying. Intuition is plugged into the universe, and sometimes the head is not."

It's a trap, Nayla thought, this is a trap.

"Keep going. Not much further!" the head Interceptor said. "If you keep on crawling, just a bit, you will be free."

Nayla started to crawl backwards.

"No! No! Forwards!" the head Interceptor said, starting to squirm in her arms. "It's not far at all until you can get to the original tunnel for your escape."

Nayla kept backing up, and the head Interceptor started trying to bite her. It nearly succeeded, it became very strong and ferocious all of a sudden, and as Nayla kept crawling backwards she felt a flood of little hands begin to push her from behind so that she slid forwards again.

"Keep pushing!" the head Interceptor said. "We will have her soon!"

They kept pushing Nayla and they began to squeeze her forward. She could barely do anything to stop them, there was no space for her to struggle.

"Keep going!" the head Interceptor said.

Nayla became angry again.

She could not struggle backwards, but she still had her hands on the head Interceptor. She began to strangle him.

"You will suffocate before anything happens to me," Nayla said.

She started to squeeze his neck tightly, and the Interceptor couldn't breathe.

It was trying to say something, and Nayla loosened her grip.

"Keep pushing!" the head Interceptor shouted, and so Nayla squeezed her hands around its neck as hard as she could, while she was pushed further and further along a tunnel that seemed to have a very dark space at the end.

*

"We can't risk going in the water after her," Takashi said to Myasako. They were running through the forest side by side. "We have to get back home."

"Well where could she be?"

"I do not know," Takashi said. "Somewhere underground, I feel, but I am not sure where. All I know is that we must return back home."

"Where's the Mountain Man gone?" Myasako said.

"I do not know," Takashi said.

The two ninjas ran together, through the woods, in the direction of the Seishin Mountain.

*

As Nayla continued to be squeezed through the narrow tunnel by a team of Interceptors pushing her from behind, she threw the head Interceptor in her hands as far forwards as she could. The head Interceptor was drowsy from just being strangled, and it went spinning off into the distance and disappeared into the darkness. She heard it yelling, and its yells gradually got quieter, as if it was falling over a ledge.

Now Nayla had both hands free to use. She dug her hands into the rocks of the tunnel that were underneath her, and she span herself around so that she was on her back. Then with the little amount of room she had, she began to kick at the Interceptors.

Some were getting squashed in between her legs and the walls of the tunnel, and they were starting to bite her.

Once one began to bite, they all began to bite, and it felt as if hundreds of little teeth were biting and pushing, trying to force her further along the tunnel.

She resisted a while longer, and then decided she was fighting a losing battle. She squirmed back on to her front, and began to crawl in the direction they were pushing her. What she did not know, is that the Interceptors had a very major flaw. They always wanted to stop their prey from doing what it wanted to do, no matter what it wanted to do. They had an element of cruelty within them that never liked to see their prey satisfied. They harvested energy from suffering, not from joy.

As Nayla crawled away from them, towards the darkness in the distance, she heard an Interceptor from behind her begin to call out.

"Stop biting her. She's trying to escape! Pull her back!"

The Interceptors started to try to grab at her feet and trouser legs, but Nayla kicked them away as they tried to gain a grip. Pulling was much harder than pushing, and soon Nayla was scurrying along this tunnel, to see what awaited her at the end.

"Stop her! Stop her! Seal off the tunnel!" another Interceptor shouted.

Nayla heard something shifting in the darkness ahead of her.

Nayla was confused at the behaviour of the Interceptors. It was as if they had a madness inside them, but a madness she could exploit.

"I want to come back in and stay with you!" Nayla shouted back at the Interceptors. "Let me stay underground with all of you."

"No!" they all shouted.

Another Interceptor shouted over the rest of them and said:

"No, no we won't have you living here, especially not if you want it. No, certainly not. No."

"Exit the tunnel!" the Interceptors all shouted, and Nayla heard a mass fleeing of Interceptors scurrying away behind her.

"Now!" the same Interceptor shouted. "Evacuate the creature so that she may not stay!"

Nayla heard something else shifting around her, and suddenly the entire floor of the tunnel gave way, and Nayla was falling through a darkness that seemed to want to keep her hidden forever.

Yield

Yielding to the greater force allows greater power to flow through us.

Chapter 19 - The Liberation Root

When Martin was walking home from school later that day, he was talking with Harry about what had been happening over the past few weeks.

"I don't believe it," Harry said. "It all sounds too unreal."

"I'm telling the truth," said Martin. "You don't have to believe me, but I can always show you some time."

"I don't think so," Harry said. "My mum has always told me to keep out of the woods."

As they continued to talk, they heard a voice call from behind them.

"Martin?"

Martin and Harry turned around. It was Arthur Muldridge, walking up to them with a timid look on his face.

"Yes?" Martin said. Martin no longer had any fear of Arthur. Not only was Martin much more confident in himself, but Arthur looked like a different person now.

"I was...I was just wondering...although you probably won't want to...would you want to come to my house some time this week, after school? You can come too, Harry. My dad said he has something to show you, something that the..." Arthur's voice went very quiet and he looked around to make sure no one else was listening. "...Something that the Garganfan asked him about."

Martin was surprised that Arthur was mentioning the Garganfan. Arthur looked around again and kept talking.

"He wanted me to ask you – bring the Garganfan too. My dad's been working on this for the past few weeks and he's ready to show it now."

Martin thought about it for a moment.

"I don't know," Martin said. "Your dad might be alright now, but he caused us a huge amount of trouble. He tried to do something terrible to my mum at his house, and because of him she was badly hurt in the forest. I don't think I want to get involved with him, or you."

"Okay," Arthur said, "well...will you at least tell the Garganfan it's ready? My father says it's ready for him, and he wants the Garganfan to come and see it. You're invited too, of course, but you don't have to come if you don't want."

"Okay," Martin said.

Arthur smiled, nodded, turned and walked back off

down the road, where he got into the back of a long and luxurious-looking car.

"I'm not going, no way," Harry said as he and Martin began to walk down the road.

"Scared?" Martin asked.

"I'm not scared," Harry said, fidgeting his arms. "I just...I just don't want to go."

"Okay," said Martin. "But even if you *were* scared, there's nothing wrong with that. That's another thing I've learned. There's nothing wrong with feeling fear."

The two friends walked off together down the road, and Martin wondered what Jacobson had been working on.

*

"I don't want to go, I don't want to go to his house. That's where he tried to kidnap my mother, before Myasako saved her, I don't care if he's been demonstralised, I don't want to forgive him."

"Why not?" the Garganfan said. He and Martin were standing in the forest amongst the trees.

"Because he doesn't deserve my forgiveness," Martin said. "He shouldn't be let off the hook like that. If I forgive him, it means what he did was okay."

175

The Garganfan sat down on an old tree stump.

"Are you sure that's what it means?" the Garganfan said.

Martin stayed standing. "Yes," he said.

The Garganfan paused for a while and looked around at the trees.

"You know, forgiveness isn't really about freeing the other person. It's about freeing yourself. You never have to go to Jacobson's house in your life, I understand that, but if you hold an unforgiveness in your heart, you will always be a prisoner to someone else's past actions, the actions carried out by the darkness that lived inside of them."

Martin thought about it for a while.

"Well even if I wanted to forgive him, I don't know how to," Martin said.

"That's because you don't want to forgive him, and you still believe what everyone else believes – that forgiveness means that the person is more likely to do the same bad thing again."

Martin looked at the ground, and sat down next to the Garganfan.

"Forgiveness means you free yourself from the past, and you free yourself from all the darkness you have encountered in the world," the Garganfan said. "If you forgive Jacobson for what he did, that doesn't affect whether or not he will do it again. It just gives you your own energy back, rather than tying it to a bad memory."

Martin could feel a little lightness begin to emerge inside of him, but he still had barriers to ever really letting go of the past.

"Okay," Martin said, "thanks. I'm still not going to his house though."

"Then I will go alone," the Garganfan said.

*

"Why won't you tell me what it is? Maybe I would come if I knew what Jacobson has been making," Martin said. He had been walking through the forest with the Garganfan for ten minutes, wondering what Jacobson had been up to.

"Because I don't know," the Garganfan said. "I asked him to *stop* making something, not to make something else. I feel he has gone against my request in some way. I will have to see what it is for myself. Now, there's something here I want to show you."

The Garganfan stopped walking, kneeled down, and began to brush away at some of the leaves on the ground.

"It is here somewhere," the Garganfan said. "I can feel it."

"Feel what? What is it?" Martin asked.

"The Liberation Root. They are in season."

"The what?"

"Have you never read about it? It's a rare root that becomes edible once a year. Around this time, there is a small amount that emerges out of the ground, ready for eating. If it isn't eaten, it withers away."

"Well why are we looking for it?" Martin said, watching the Garganfan gently brushing through the leaves.

"It's for you, if you want it. I thought you might want it to get over any pain that you are still storing from the past. It gets rid of it for you."

"Is it safe?"

"Yes. Unless you find danger in releasing yourself from pain and resentments. Most people think that's a dangerous thing to do. Here it is."

The Garganfan broke off a small green root from the ground with ease, and he raised it to his eye level.

"Perfect," he said.

Martin hadn't moved.

"You don't have to eat it," the Garganfan said. "It's up to you."

He handed Martin the little green root. It was heavier and rougher than Martin expected.

"What will happen if I eat it?" Martin said.

"It will take you deep into the recesses of your mind where your deepest fears and resentments are living. Then it will allow you to open the doors of resistance that you have been layering on top of them, so that they may be released."

"Will it hurt?"

"For a moment, yes."

Martin held the root. He wasn't even aware that he was carrying much pain from the past, from the harassment and attack of Jacobson Muldridge. He put the root in his pocket and said he would think about it.

"Very well," the Garganfan said. "But remember, you don't need the root. You can free yourself by using your own power that always lives within you."

"Okay," Martin said. "Well I need to go home now, my dinner will be ready soon."

"Very well," the Garganfan said. "I will walk you out."

As the two companions walked together through the woods, Martin was suddenly aware of a heavy weight that was living within his chest. As he felt it, it felt like darkness, with images of his mother being hurt and his family being put at risk by a man with no morality. He noticed, strangely, that in an unusual way, he slightly enjoyed the outrage of it all.

He liked it, very slightly. It gave him something to think about, something to resist, something to object against, and as he realised that his mind had the habit of focussing on all the bad things that had been happening recently, he started to relax.

He didn't have to do this anymore. He didn't have to carry the past around like a weight on his back, condemning everyone for everything they had done. He wanted to be free, he wanted to feel how he used to feel before Jacobson had tried to hunt him and his mother down.

As he saw the edge of the forest in the distance, he felt a wonderful lightness begin to surround him, and then this lightness filtered in through his body and started to break apart every piece of darkness that had ever lived inside of him.

As they reached the edge of the forest, Martin took

out the Liberation Root from his pocket. He handed it to the Garganfan.

"I don't think I need this now," Martin said. "You can pass it on to someone else who needs it. See you tomorrow, let's go and see what Jacobson has been making."

The Garganfan took the Liberation Root and watched Martin walk away towards his house.

The Garganfan looked down at the root, held it for a moment, and said the words:

"Thank you."

Forgiveness

Forgiveness is a path to freedom.

Chapter 20 - The Gatekeeper

As Nayla continued to fall through a cold darkness, she could hear the Interceptors start to cheer from above.

"She's gone!"

"We did it!"

"Hooray!"

She heard their cheers grow quieter as she continued to fall, and she was falling for so long that she started to become comfortable.

She could hear the air whizzing past her ears, but since she couldn't see anything, as time went on she started to feel as if she was just standing still, without a floor.

She was sure that if she was to land, her body would break, and she realised that there was nothing she could do about it, except to go soft.

She relaxed her mind and body, and she asked the question:

"Where am I?"

Immediately in front of her some faint writing appeared. It said:

"The portal of transport."

"How do I get back home?" she asked.

"You must request, and pass the test."

Nayla stared at the writing.

"Okay," she said. "I would like to go back to Kuyasaki's dojo behind the Seishin Mountain, where my mother is."

"Very well."

Suddenly Nayla was on solid ground, in a dimly-lit cave with a dirty floor.

She stood up, looked to her right, and out hobbled an old, decrepit-looking creature carrying a rolled-up piece of paper and a walking stick. It was not a human, but had two arms and two legs.

"Questions!" the creature said. It had green skin which was mostly covered by a dark hood and cloak.

"Questions!" it said again, hobbling further towards her and gradually sitting down by the wall.

"Three questions you must answer correct in order to pass my test. I am the Gatekeeper, and from where I have emerged is your portal back to your desired location. But only I may activate it, if I am satisfied with your answers."

"Okay," Nayla said. She was still looking around to make sure that nothing was to jump out at her. She had a hand on one of her daggers.

"Question number one!" the Gatekeeper said, reading off his piece of paper.

"What seeks to dwell inside the rocks but can't ever be stopped? What wears away at everything, but can nourish or rot?"

Nayla looked around at the rocky walls. They were glistening.

The Gatekeeper was staring at her with one of its piercing eyes from under its hood.

"Water," she said.

"Hmm," the Gatekeeper said. "Very well."

"Question number two! What force is there more powerful than any in the land? The force that can enlighten, as abundant as the sand? A force that comes from deep within, that many seek to hide? The one that brings a clarity, and supports the rest of life?"

"I don't know," Nayla said.

"Then you are stuck," the Gatekeeper said, smiling.

"How many guesses do I have?"

"Unlimited. You are here for an eternity otherwise."

Nayla thought back to her past. Only darkness was there. She thought of her father, and although she still resented him for what he had done, deep down she felt a love for him, for who he truly was behind the layers of evil.

"Love?" Nayla said.

"Correct," the Gatekeeper said, resentfully returning to his piece of paper.

"Question number three will not be so easy. What is it that seeks but never finds? What pretends to have eyes but always is blind? What is it that strangles so many a person? It has no arms, it has no legs, it isn't a serpent. It acts like a guardian of all who will have it, but instead it attracts its likeness through habit...

"What is it that lures the mind of many, a devil that halts the coming of plenty? A beast that lives in the heart and mind, a cloud that makes abundance blind?"

Nayla didn't say anything for a while.

"Any other clues?" she asked.

"When it arises it isn't a problem, unless you think it will solve your problems. Have it in flashes and at the right times, then it can fuel you in disastrous times. But keep it inside as a mental projection, then it will hurt you to teach you a lesson."

"And what's the lesson?" Nayla said.

"That it keeps you shackled to the outcomes that you don't want," the Gatekeeper said, putting his paper down on his legs.

"Fear," Nayla said. "The answer is fear."

The Gatekeeper sighed and looked at his feet. Nayla saw loneliness in him for a moment. Then he spoke.

"You will be transported to the nearest emergence hole, at the top of the Seishin Mountain. Exit the cave immediately, be very quiet and make your way home. My questions need to be harder!"

The Gatekeeper picked up his walking stick and slammed it into the ground with fury, and Nayla's body was sucked into the dark portal ahead of her that the Gatekeeper had emerged from, and she hoped that she was heading back home.

Hope

Stay true to your hopes,
and allow them to become living realities.

Chapter 21 - Jacobson's Creation

The next day after school, Martin approached the estate of Jacobson Muldridge, through the woods, with the Garganfan. Harry had decided to stay home.

They could see the huge house in the distance across a field that led away from the forest.

"What's this all about? What did you ask Jacobson to stop doing?" Martin asked again.

"You'll see," the Garganfan said. "But I have a very uncomfortable feeling about all of this, as if Jacobson's mind has hijacked my request and turned it into something else."

The two friends walked across the field towards the house, and Jacobson could see them from the window of his piano room.

"They're here! They're here!" Jacobson started shouting. "Everyone get ready!"

All of his members of staff began to gather outside the house to greet the two. They formed a tunnel of people leading towards the door. When Martin and the Garganfan arrived, they were greeted by a round of applause.

"Welcome!" Jacobson said, walking out of the

house to shake the two by the hand. "I'm so glad you could come. Follow me."

"Where's Arthur?" Martin said, still with an element of distrust.

"He's just inside," Jacobson said, leading them in through the tunnel of staff. "Here he is."

"Hello," Arthur said, standing inside the door. "Thanks for coming."

Martin noticed that everywhere was spotless. Everything was shining and clean and fantastic, and Jacobson started to lead them through the house.

"It's not too far," Jacobson said. "Follow me."

They followed Jacobson as he led them through grand corridors with golden pillars and fine paintings on the walls. Martin couldn't believe this was just one man's house.

After a while of walking, with the Garganfan ignoring all paintings and golden pillars, they reached a red door.

"This isn't quite what you've asked for," Jacobson said to the Garganfan, "but I've had my team working flat-out to get it done. I've gone a step further than what you requested. It's the least I could do in return for you saving my son from those Bodysnatchers."

The Garganfan still wasn't speaking. Martin had never seen him look so uncomfortable. It was as if he already knew what was behind that red door.

"Are you ready?" Jacobson said

The Garganfan did not respond, and neither did Martin, but as Jacobson opened that red door, Martin had an unexplained sense of doom rise up in his chest, and he felt his entire body go cold.

"It's ready," Jacobson said.

The End

Book 4 out now...

Continue The Adventure!

Find out what happens to Nayla after she emerges from the portal of transport, and see what happens when Jacobson unleashes his new invention on the world...

Book 4 out now on Amazon!

Get the full 6-book series on Amazon now, and join the adventures of Martin, Myasako and Nayla...

Out Now On Amazon:

Coming Soon:

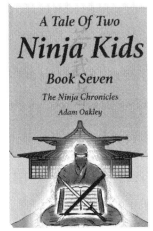

194

More Adventures

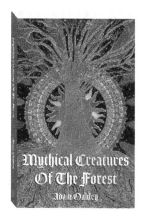

Discover more stories about the Garganfan and the Mountain Man...

Meet the Dundenbeast, the Shapeshifter, Heelog, the Treekeeper, the Feasting Tree, the Pikaloo, the Healybug and many others...

Join Dr Bernard J. Hoothfellow as he embarks on his mission to discover all the creatures in the forest that no one believes to be real.

Adventure awaits.

"Mythical Creatures Of The Forest"

Out now on Amazon

Inspirational short stories for ages 8 and up...

Meet the boy who could not worry, the man who has become free from labels, the mysterious bear who has wisdom to share, and the frog who has discovered the secret to lasting joy.

These are great stories for parents and children to read together or alone, and each have their own message for a more fulfilling life.

"Happiness Is Inside: 25 Inspirational Stories For Greater Peace Of Mind"

Out now on Amazon.

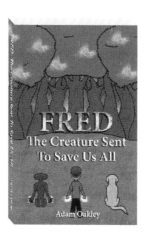

When Wallace finds a strange creature emerging out of his back garden, he decides it must be an alien. Little does he know that the creature named Fred has been sent from deep within the Earth to put a stop to the burning of the Chatamanga Rainforest, and he needs Wallace's help.

Together Fred and Wallace go on a mission to try to save the rainforest from burning, and when they discover who is really behind the fires, they discover a whole new world...

A journey of adventure, self-discovery, and environmental protection, join the adventures of Fred and get the book for yourself or a loved one!

"Fred: The Creature Sent To Save Us All"

Out now on Amazon

*If you enjoyed this book, **please leave a review on Amazon** – it helps the book to reach more people!*

Thank you.

Follow Adam on social media here:

@ninjakidsbook

@adamoakleybooks

About The Author

Adam is an author from the UK who loves to write all different kinds of books.

He writes books about inner peace, inner power, and loves writing stories that feel like stepping into other realms.

He spends his time writing, doing martial arts, growing organic food and spending time with his family.

He hopes you loved reading the book, and he is grateful for any young readers or parents who can leave a review on Amazon to help the book reach more people.

He thanks you for your support, and is always available to contact via one of his websites:

www.AdamOakleyBooks.com

www.InnerPeaceNow.com

Manufactured by Amazon.ca
Bolton, ON

25835080R00114